PENGUIN BOOKS

THE BIRD OF NIGHT

Susan Hill was born in Scarborough, Yorkshire, in 1942. She was educated at grammar schools there and in Coventry, and studied at King's College, London. Her works include *Gentleman and Ladies*, *A Change for the Better*, *I'm the King of the Castle* (Somerset Maugham Prize), *The Albatross and Other Stories* (John Llewelyn Rhys Memorial Prize), *Strange Meeting*, *The Bird of Night* (Whitbread Award), *A Bit of Singing and Dancing*, *In the Springtime of the Year*, *The Woman in Black*, *Lanterns Across the Snow* and *Air and Angels*, as well as the illustrated *Shakespeare Country*, *The Spirit of the Cotswolds*, *Through the Garden Gate* and *Through the Kitchen Window*. She has also written books for children, *One Night at a Time*, *Mother's Magic*, *Can It Be True?* (Smarties Prize) and *Suzy's Shoes*, and two autobiographical books, *The Magic Apple Tree* and *Family*. In addition she has edited Thomas Hardy's *The Distracted Preacher and Other Tales* for the Penguin Classics. She has also edited *The Penguin Book of Modern Women's Short Stories* and is a regular broadcaster and book reviewer.

Susan Hill is married to the Shakespeare scholar Stanley Wells. They have two daughters and live in the Oxfordshire countryside.

Susan Hill

The Bird of Night

Penguin Books

PENGUIN BOOKS

Published by the Penguin Group
Penguin Books Ltd, 27 Wrights Lane, London W8 5TZ, England
Penguin Books USA Inc., 375 Hudson Street, New York, New York 10014, USA
Penguin Books Australia Ltd, Ringwood, Victoria, Australia
Penguin Books Canada Ltd, 10 Alcorn Avenue, Toronto, Ontario, Canada M4V 3B2
Penguin Books (NZ) Ltd, 182–190 Wairau Road, Auckland 10, New Zealand

Penguin Books Ltd, Registered Offices: Harmondsworth, Middlesex, England

First published in Great Britain by Hamish Hamilton 1972
First published in the United States of America
by Saturday Review Press 1973
Published in Penguin Books 1976
10 9

Printed in England by Clays Ltd, St Ives plc
Set in Linotype Pilgrim

For William Plomer

'I am an old man who has experienced much.
I have also read books and studied and
pondered and tried to fathom eternal truth.
Much good has been shown to me and some
evil and the good has never been perfect.
There is always some fault in the angelic
song, some stammer in the divine speech. So
that the Devil still has something to do with
every human consignment to this planet of
earth.

   'Oh, what have I done? Oh, what have I
done? Confusion, so much is confusion. I
have tried to guide others rightly, but I have
been lost on the infinite sea. Who has blessed
me? Who saved me?'

— From Benjamin Britten's opera Billy Budd,
*libretto by Eric Crozier and E. M. Forster by
permission of Boosey and Hawkes Music
Publishers Ltd.*

The Bird of Night

Once, during a summer we spent at Kerneham, Francis locked himself in the church for the whole of a night. I found him there, at five o'clock the next morning, huddled up beneath the pulpit. It was cold. He could not feel safe anywhere else, he said, and then he began to weep, as so often happened, and shouted at me through his weeping, to understand the truth, that he deserved to be locked up, why would I not admit that and see to it, why had I driven him to do it for himself?

That is what I remembered this morning but I do not know why one bubble should break upon the surface rather than another. I should be content that I remember.

At half past three, Mrs Mumford will come up from the village and put the kettle on, it will be tea-time. As I get old, I discover that I mark out each day like this, it is upsetting beyond reason when there is a change in the routine.

But it is still too early, Mrs Mumford will not come yet. If I half-close my eyes, the flowers dance.

It is when I look at my hands that I believe I am an old man. Not even this awkward business of walking so slowly on two sticks brings home the truth to me so much as the sight of these hands. They are identical to the hands of my father, and my grandfather too, and those I remember only as old hands, the skin almost transparent over raised veins, the knobs of the joints pushing up beneath. As a child, I stared at my father's hands.

I cannot reconcile them, now, to myself.

This morning – was it only this morning? – one of the young men came. This one had red hair and very pale, long, long fingers; he waved them about in the air as he spoke. If I half-closed my eyes – it is a way of cutting myself off from their

7

talk – I saw that his hands were like the fronds of weed that lie just under the clear water of the river that runs across the marshes here, they undulated in such a way. The flesh was greenish.

I loathed him, he was an effete young man. He was ingratiating. He called me Sir, in a way that was impertinent and, after lunch, he picked surreptitiously at the back of his teeth with one of the long, pale fingers.

I generally have to give them lunch, it is such a long way that they come. Oh, and I wish that they would not.

He said, 'I am very anxious to be given access to papers.'

'There are no papers.'

'Oh come, sir, you can tell the truth to me! There must be papers – and surely you owe it to his memory – to scholarship . . .'

That is what they all say.

'Naturally, you can trust absolutely in my discretion.'

And that is what they all say.

Then, sometimes, they begin to bully me, or to wheedle, they treat me as though I were wicked, or weak in the head. I have listened to them all.

'Surely there are diaries, letters – notebooks.'

'There are no papers.'

I can scarcely speak to him, I am falling asleep. I have forgotten his name hours ago.

I open my eyes. Behind his head, through the window, I can see the silver line of the estuary.

He is from a new university, of which I have never heard. He leans forward eagerly, suddenly, and I see the pale freckles on his pale skin. He spits a little in his desire to be sincere.

'This is something I feel in my bones that I must do. Can you not understand that, sir? I know that I have an affinity of some kind with him, I feel a *closeness*.'

That is too much, that I cannot bear, at last he has made me angry. But I am courteous enough, I do not shout. I think, they cannot touch him, or me, none of them.

Sometimes, a day comes without even a letter and then I can believe we are still in that world which was private to us, that none of them know anything about Francis. I live now for such days. Then I can sit here, or walk as far as I am able, to where the path begins to curve across the marshes, I can look back and see everything clearly, I can remember the truth.

Oh, but each day they come, the terrible letters.

For instance, one wants to prove that Francis was not mad at all. Or that his madness was the result of a virus dormant in the spine. Or that he was mad in precisely the same fashion as George III, or the poet Christopher Smart or the poet John Clare.

Or in exactly the opposite way to each of these.

There will be one who is preparing a new critical analysis of the early poems and the war poems, the two long poems, the last fragments. He wrote so little, God knows, the volumes are so thin, I can hold them together in one of my hands, how can they have spawned all these other volumes which commentate? And it had all begun in his lifetime, the files are here. But to me, these are parasites, they feed off his work, as the inquisitive would feed off my memories. And perhaps there are a hundred books and articles about which I am told nothing. How I wish to God they would all tell me nothing!

That is why I came to live here when I retired thirteen years ago. It is remote, it is rather hard to find. I was so accustomed to running away, to hiding, during the nineteen years of our life together. Besides, I have no inclination for company now. My house is a mile away from any other. Mrs Mumford walks from the village.

And I live here because it is near the sea. And because Francis was happy here. And because it is beautiful.

I shall die here. I do not intend to let them take me away to any home or institution. I shall manage, in the best way I can.

Now, I can scarcely remember the young man who came this morning. They tease me a little, that is all, they irritate, and I twitch them away, as I would get rid of a fly.

I am remote, but they still come, they invite themselves and drive fifty or five hundred miles in their cars to see me. Each time, I swear that I will never admit another. Then, there is always a moment of guilt, that perhaps I am wrong, for who am I to stand in the way of fame? Perhaps the young man was right, I am being unjust to Francis. And so I reply to another letter, and they come.

'There must have been diaries – letters – notebooks.'

'There are no papers.'

The papers are here, the diaries and the notebooks with their soft, shiny black covers, here under my hand, and the letters in the blue case. These are mine. I shall write what is to be written. That was the understanding between us.

It is four o'clock. Mrs Mumford brings a tray from the house. I have tea and lemon-cake and the scent comes towards me from the bed of white phlox just behind my chair.

In the sun, when my bones do not ache, I can forget that I am old.

*

'The first occasion on which I met Francis
Croft was at a house party in Sussex a few years
after the Great War.'

That is what I had written.

It is quite late at night. I am sitting in my study, which has a door opening on to the garden. I can smell the phlox even more strongly than before, and the honeysuckle which falls in a great, loose swathe down the west wall of the house. I am so much more aware, these days, of scents and sounds, of the minute wrinkles and creases in the surface of the day. When I was young, I took them for granted, though probably I would always have said that I appreciated them to the full.

I knew nothing about them, nothing. It is only now, when I am eighty years old, that the lessons I absorbed in the course of my life with Francis are truly learned, and at last I understand their value. Though it may seem a triviality, that I am aware of the scent of flowers.

It is high summer. It is a warm night. Mrs Mumford has gone, they are all gone. Now I am happiest. Because there is a slight, warm breeze coming towards the house, I can just hear the rasp of the sea as it pulls back down the shingle, like wind moving through the branches of elm trees.

I do not often go as far as the sea. Rarely even as far as the estuary. I am content to know that they are there. I used to sit for hours watching the sea birds, and the birds which nest further inland among the marshes. I am too crippled to do so now. It is something I miss.

I have a glass of claret on my desk, the last of the bottle I drank with my supper. I have one of the five cigarettes which I smoke each day freshly alight in my hand. I am in that mood which Francis most appreciated.

And I have begun to write and at once realized that it is no beginning. For those are the neat, dry, formal words of a chronicler, they would lead us into 'A Biographical and Appreciative Essay on the poet Francis Croft'.

God knows, whatever I am writing, it is not that. No tight, careful little structure will contain the man as I knew him. Though, when I think about that, I see that it is very remarkable. For when he was writing, in full possession of all his wits, either before the madness touched him, or later, in the periods of calm and sanity between, he was above all a poet who believed passionately that content was inseparable from form. What he always tried to make were beautiful and meaningful structures. He wrote a number of sonnets. But even more often, the structures were entirely original, very complex, and meticulously worked out. He was a man of violent feelings, a man of beliefs and passions, he was a poet with a vision, he had everything, everything to say. But he meant to contain it, to make beautiful patterns.

I have opened one of the notebooks in front of me and I find copious quotations from *The Six-Cornered Snowflake*, by the seventeenth-century German mathematician Johann Kepler.

For instance:

There must be some definite cause why, whenever snow begins to fall, its initial formations invariably display the shape of a six-cornered starlet. For if it happens by chance, why do they not fall just as well with five corners, or seven?

(The translation is mine, Francis read the book in the original Latin, and there is no English version, though there are several available in German.)

Further down, after a note about Kubla Khan, there is another observation from Kepler.

Pomegranates, honeycombs and snowflakes all built upon same rhomboidal principle.

Francis read Kepler constantly, it was one of the few books he always took with him when he went abroad. There were times when he had me read it to him, during some of the agitated phases of his madness. The sound of the familiar Latin, the ideas Kepler put forward about the perfect construction of the snowflake, never failed to soothe him. Then, he would occasionally buy a pomegranate, cut it in half, and leave the open sections on his desk, admiring their beautiful internal structure, though he greatly disliked the taste of the fruit.

So that, even when his poems appear most free, there is always a skeleton, a highly sophisticated pattern of rhythm and stress, holding the piece together. The only formless writings, apart from quick jottings in the notebooks, are those fragments he scrawled down when he was at the farthest point of his madness. They were many of them burned by him one terrible night at Kerneham, to which I shall return. Those which remain have never been published. But even in these, I have occasionally discerned some sad evidence of his desperate attempt to 'make a pattern', to order his turbulent thoughts and the words on the paper.

Besides, he himself was so beautifully fashioned, he had such good proportions to his body, he satisfied the eye, though never because he was especially neat or spruce. And certainly I do not say that he was handsome. But there was always the impression that he had been carefully made, he did not look, as some men do, that he had come together by accident, all anyhow.

Somewhere in the heathland beyond the back of the house, a nightjar churrs softly over and over again, I imagine it turning its head from side to side as it calls, so that the churr comes now loudly, now as though from far away, and when it flies, there will be the quick whip-crack sound of its wings. I listen to it for some moments. They tell me that nightjars are becoming rare in this part of the country.

I realize that I have more than begun, I have plunged on too far ahead, I have already lost any sense of pattern. But that is right, that cannot be as bad as the pompous, meaningless attempt at a formal 'beginning', of that Francis would have so greatly disapproved. I am ashamed that I could have written it.

The truth is that I cannot make a formal shape or a progression from A to Z of Francis's life, or of my friendship with him, I must set down what he was and what became of him, and of me – for it is about us both that I must write, I cannot hope to exclude myself – as it seems best, as things come to me.

I have said that he was an artist concerned with form. But it was the spontaneousness of his thought and of his approach to life which impresses most. What one becomes acquainted with, reading his work, even if one did not know him, is a quickness of mind, a brilliance, together always with a depth of feeling, and a passionate commitment to his vision. His work overflows, even while it is contained.

I am not like Francis. I am another kind of man. My first instinct would be to write the formal biographical study which I began, that is what I would do most competently. But it is not competence that is required of me.

I was trained as a Classicist. I became an Egyptologist: a writer of learned footnotes. I spent some time, before I met Francis, in the British Museum, and I returned to it, after his death, for thirteen years. I could write a memoir of him which would be as dry as tomb dust.

But I shall not. I shall trust to instinct. I shall let down a bucket and spill out whatever I bring up across the page, for this is what Francis would have approved.

It is not an easy story, it is a most terrible story to write, I shall not have the courage to spend years over the telling of it. I am an old man.

Every day now, my mind fills to overflowing with memories. I sit in a chair. I walk a little on two sticks. I know that the only important years of my life were those – can it only be a quarter of the total? – during which I knew Francis. I was with him throughout the period of his best work, throughout the course

of his madness, until his death. I shall write what has to be
written.

*

On the Saturday afternoon, I went into the library and there
was Francis Croft, to whom I had been introduced, and taken a
mild dislike, the previous evening.

She had said, 'This is our *celebrity*,' and he had laughed, not
contradicting her.

He was immensely tall, several inches taller than me; he
balanced upon his long legs like an avocet and he leaned forward; he was round-shouldered with stooping. He was short-
sighted, his hair was very thick and very straight, the colour of
tobacco. There was a purple birth-mark above his right eye-
brow.

I wanted to put him in his place, I wished that I could say I
had not heard of him. But he had survived the trenches of
Flanders and his war poems were already published and widely
praised.

'I'm afraid I read very little poetry.'

He smiled, an indulgent, prideful smile.

Later, he reminded me of what I had so pompously said.

I tried to defend myself. 'It was perfectly true at the time.'

'Oh, but that's not the point at all, you know, the point is,
you really shouldn't have *said* it, I was frightfully offended.'

He had a rather slow, precise way of speaking and, except
when he was ill, his voice was very soft. When he talked for a
long time, or read something to me, it had a hypnotic quality.
But in the bouts of terror and despair and delirium, he would
cry out and then there would be a harsh edge to his voice, he
would roar like an animal.

I went into the library.

'Hullo? Oh good, I'm glad it's you, Harvey, you can stand
and hold the ladder for me.'

He was at the top of it, his tall, thin body was bending like a
cane towards me.

'I'm surprised you remember my name.'

'Oh yes, I'm rather good at names.'

'I see.' I heard myself, stiff and rather sour, unused to being
addressed by my Christian name without invitation.

'Now do hold on to this ladder, I'm looking for Blake and I'm terrified of heights really, I'm perfectly certain the thing's going to give way.'

I held on to it, my face set politely.

It had begun to snow. I stood in the quiet, dark room and watched soft, fat flakes come spinning down, I watched the lawn and the gravel drive give way to the encroaching whiteness. There is a brilliance, a dazzle about snow, which has always pleased me.

'How do you like our hostess? She's really pretty harmless, it seems to me. I thought she was a dragon to begin with. A youngish dragon.'

I looked up. He was sitting on the top step, his knees tucked up almost to his chin, balancing a pair of huge brown books, one of which he had opened. I resented being made to stand there like a lackey, keeping him steady.

'Have you known her for long?'

'Some years, yes.'

My brother had been to school with hers. When she had married, she had set about making a name for herself as a Famous Hostess. She was succeeding.

'I scarcely know her at all, I really can't think what I'm doing here. I was having tea with a friend in Oxford and she arrived, and asked me almost at once. I was a bit put out. I mean, I don't usually – but I do like it, I must say, it's so fearfully sybaritic and so marvellously *dull*. I do adore dullness – really one gets sufficient dramas and diversions in the outside world, don't you think?'

I thought him affected. I understand now that it was all nervousness, I often heard him talk like this in strange company, later on, but he never did it again with me.

'Actually, I was only looking for Blake as an after-thought. I came in here for a book about owls. I mean they do seem to have absolutely everything. Do you know about owls at all?'

'Long-eared, short-eared, tawny, little or barn?'

'Oh my God, that's marvellous, that's what I want – a *list*. I make lists of everything all the time. I adore lists. Are you an ornithologist?'

'Occasionally.'

He seemed to find me amusing, there was a grin on his long pale face which he was trying unsuccessfully to bring under control.

I said, 'There are a couple of tawnies nesting in the ivy over-growing a dead chestnut at the bottom of the farm path.'

'Ah, I heard them last night. I wondered where they were.' He paused. 'What a *wise* man you do seem to be, Harvey.'

He was looking down on me benignly. I was, in fact, a year older than him, but he made me feel foolishly young, in spite of what he said. I tried to remember what I had read about him, what sort of opinion of him the world had. He baffled me. But already the mild dislike of him had given way to amiability. I thought that he was trying very hard to be pleasing.

He said, 'The owl is an augur of death, I suppose you know that?'

'No.'

'Owls, ravens, hedgehogs and snakes. In Shropshire they're called Gilly-whites. Or sometimes Oolerts. Isn't Gilly-Whites a beautiful name?'

'Do you come from Shropshire?'

'No.' He sounded displeased then. I was to find out after-wards how much he disliked having to answer direct personal questions. Time and again, I have seen him dazzle a single person, or half a dozen, talking almost non-stop and barraging them with question after question, all to divert attention and curiosity from himself.

After a moment, I left the ladder and walked away across the polished wood floor to the tall window. The snow had completely covered the lawn now, the branches of the trees were beginning to sag with the weight of it and the sky was swollen and curiously orange. For some reason I felt as though I were detached from my body, I watched myself watching the falling snow. I felt immensely calm.

> 'But night soon came and the pale, white moon
> Rolled high up in the skies.
> And the grey brown owl flew away in her cowl,
> With her large, round, shining eyes.'

I stood there, listening to him. He said, 'The world is changed.

Now it has put on a white mask like a surgeon. If you do that no one can tell what you are thinking.'

'They cannot anyway.'

'Oh, don't you believe it, my dear, *I* know, I always know. I know what you are thinking now.'

'Nothing, particularly.'

'You were wishing I would leave you in peace.'

'No!' For I was not.

Inside the room it was too dark for us to see each other. There was only the glint of his spectacles at the top of the ladder. Outside, there was the queer, pale radiance of the snow.

'We could find some Wellington boots and tread about in it a little, after tea.'

I remember that I felt suddenly suspicious, I felt alarmed, there was too much about Francis Croft which I did not understand.

'I think I won't. I came in here to read.'

He chuckled. 'Ah. You're probably *very* wise.' But he said it in a strange way, so that I had no idea at all what he meant.

A few seconds later, he had come quickly down the ladder and was gone, the door bumped to behind him. The room was quite silent, then, quite dark. It went on gently snowing.

How often I must have dreamed, every night of my long life perhaps, and forgotten all of them except this one.

I was dreaming of winter. I stood in a lane beside a hawthorn hedge and the frost had laced the twigs over with delicate, brittle strands of ice, powdery snow lay balanced between. There was a puddle of water at my feet, iced over and transparent except in the centre, where it had been cracked by a single stone and the ice was meshed out in fine lines from a hollow core. Beside me stood two horses, and the breath came steaming out of their moist nostrils and froze at once upon the air, they tossed their heads and their eyes shone, I could hear the harness chinking. I had a hand on the neck of one horse, the muscle was thick and strongly fleshed, and the coat faintly sticky to my touch. The hawthorn hedge glittered.

When I close my eyes now, nearly fifty years later, I am back within that dream which preceded my walk with Francis, and though I have never dreamed it since, all the details are vividly clear to me. I told him about it. He said, 'Dreams are important.' But I did not understand this one.

I woke because someone was tapping on my door. It was just after two o'clock in the morning.

'What is it?'

'Francis.'

'Oh – well, come in, what's wrong?'

He closed the door carefully behind him, stooping down to the handle. He was fully dressed and wearing boots over his trousers and an old, dingy raincoat. Balanced on his thick hair but pulled down at each side over his ears, he wore a yellow, knitted hat. He did not apologize for waking me. When he was preoccupied with himself, marking with rising anxiety what had begun to stir inside his head, he wanted someone who might be able to divert him, whose presence might even help to ward off the worst things. Though it never worked, those things always followed, they never could be warded off, except perhaps, in those early days, for a few hours.

It was strange that then, when I knew almost nothing of him at all, I did not resent his having disturbed me. I was not an especially tolerant man. Certainly I had never been intuitively concerned with the needs of another person. I had until then led an arid and rather selfish life. But already I was aware that with Francis things would become different, I should be different, that I would not behave in any of the usual ways.

He said, 'I really must go out. I wanted you to come with me.'

'Are you ill?'

'Of course not, I am perfectly well. There is nothing wrong with me, why should there be?' He spoke not angrily, but impatiently.

I imagine that there must have been a moment when I decided whether or not to go.

Francis had turned his back upon me, his hand was twitching the curtain. He said, 'The snow has stopped falling.'

I got out of bed in silence, dressed, found a pair of strong shoes.

'Won't you need a hat? Do have this one, it was hanging

up in the cloakroom, really, I should be miserable if you caught a chill, one can catch a *fearful* chill from having cold ears.'

I shook my head and laughed suddenly, he looked so ludicrous, tall as a crane, with the knitted hat perched on top of his head.

We went down through the sleeping house. Francis opened the front door and there it was, the snow, in drifts and billows, lit by a full moon, changing the shape of everything, moulding the gateways and window ledges and gables of the house. It was deep and dry, very soft. There was no sound at all except for the muffled tread of our boots and the faint crunch as we pressed our weight down. It reflected palely back into our faces. Francis put out a hand and shook the branch of a fir tree, and the snow came toppling down, it lay like sugar along the sleeve of his coat.

We walked across both lawns, and through the pleached walk, quite unable to find or follow any of the paths, and up into the park, which surrounded the house on three sides, for twenty acres. Behind us, our footsteps led back, gleaming like a snail's trail.

It was not cold, and quite windless, the air smelled oddly sweet and dry. The horse-chestnuts and beeches of the park stood, with the snow outlining their outspread, slender arms. It creaked a little as we walked through it.

Francis had not spoken. At first, I had been bewildered by him, but now I was quite content to walk mile after mile through this silent, white moonlit world, I was grateful to him for bringing me out. There was something timeless and reminiscent of childhood, I was seeing a landscape I had never seen before and yet which seemed entirely familiar, as though I had often walked about it in my dreams.

A pace or two further on, Francis stopped. We were in the middle of the park. There was silence, and then a soft, steady whirring of wings, a humming noise as the air was caught up in eddies through the wood. Then a tawny owl appeared, moving towards us down a tunnel between the trees. Its face was white-feathered, like a helmet, the eyes enormous on either side of its hooked beak. As it passed us, the great eyes searching from side to side, it made a low throaty sound, almost a groan, and then, floating back to us through the air came the long hollow hoo-hoo. Francis turned and looked at me, and for a moment I thought that he was afraid, I saw his face pale as that of the owl, his eyes similarly huge and luminous behind the spectacles. But he only said, 'There now!'

'Yes, we were lucky.'

'Oh, I don't believe much in that sort of luck, you know.'

'What then?'

'Things just – make a pattern, don't you think?'

It was something I was often to hear him say and usually he would mean bad things, what I should have called unlucky.

'Things make a pattern.'

It began to snow again, thin, small flakes; they felt furry as they touched my bare face.

'Now we must go back, one must never try to interfere with the pattern once it has been completed – and you really should be back in bed, I feel quite guilty about you.'

I laughed.

'You see, my dear, I should have come out walking whether or not, but I like it to be *companionable* now and again. When I can.'

It was the kind of thing he said in that light, precise way of his, and which meant infinitely more than I ever guessed at the time. He had been until this time an exceptionally lonely man. But when he chose, he would also say profound things without levity, he would speak the truth out loud, most especially when it was a dark, despairing truth.

We came out of the trees, following in our own tracks, which were already disappearing under the fresh fall of snow. The house stood very clear-edged, the rose-red brick drained of its colour beneath the moon.

I knew nothing at all that night about Francis's mood, though perhaps I may just have sensed that he had 'something on his mind'. For the next twenty years, I would go in dread of this beginning, when he woke me up wanting to go out and walk, no matter where we might be. Later, when the madness had swollen up and taken him over completely, he did not want me, he would try and escape by himself, to walk blindly, and in terrible distress, anywhere, anywhere, trying to soothe himself, trying to find relief from his devils. Then, I had to go searching for him and bring him back, always afraid of what I might find, of some accident happening to him.

There was nothing of this that night in the snow, what I felt when I got back to my room was a heavy tiredness and a sense of pleasure past, an absence of any anxiety at all. I felt changed. And when I told him that, Francis looked at me in surprise, he said, 'Well, you were changed.' He believed very much in the active power of circumstance, he believed in revelation. He believed in good and, most especially, in evil, in God, but, more personally, in the Devil. Later, he told me that his heart had turned over in dread when he heard the pulsing wings through the wood and saw the ancient, hooded face of the owl. He could not explain to me why, he could never explain. But the poem which he wrote that night, and which is one of his most famous and frequently anthologized poems, is also one of the most frightening and powerful. I have read it again tonight, and I see how much of him it contains, how much of his deep sense of fate and mystery. I see that it makes something momentous out of what I thought then simply a walk through the dark countryside in snow.

But no, that is not true, for I did know, I carried with me in great fear this knowledge that the night had been of such consequence.

I remember nothing more of that weekend. We may have talked about the war. I do not even recall whether or not I met him again before the day on which we arranged to have lunch together in London. He had rooms in Oxford at that time, although he held no position at the University.

I sit all day in my garden, trying to bring small facts to the surface of my mind but they will not come. I tire myself. The sun has been obscured all day by a heat haze like gauze, the river has shrunk to a trickle covering only the grey pebbles on its bed. There are cattle just beyond my gate, they feed on the rich grass of the marshes, and now they come right to my fence, their heads hang heavy and still, and their eyes are glazed.

I have walked as far as the bend in the path. My legs are painful today, there is a burning sensation deep inside my bones. I have a sense of weariness with all that I see and hear. But I must think, I must remember, there seems so little time. My early memories of Francis are like a row of brilliantly illuminated miniatures, but only darkness lies between.

He did not keep the appointment. I know that I ordered for myself, and ate something, I know that I waited for more than an hour. And then, for the first time, I felt dread on his behalf. I was to become telepathic with regard to him and my forebodings were always justified, always confirmed. I waited in the restaurant and he did not come.

The notebooks give me an idea of what I myself was doing during these early days, for I see that Francis has copied into the inside covers of one of them some of the cartouches of the early Pharaohs on which I was working at the British Museum. I found a dry satisfaction in my subject, but Francis saw beauty in it. He spent hours at a time among my books, copying down tiny details, he said that he admired 'the pattern they made'.

His mind would have grown bored occupied as closely with the Egyptians, day after day, as mine was. But his own leaped here and there, alighting like a jackdaw upon some brightness which attracted him. When, a year or so later, the finds at the tomb of Tutankhamen became known to us, Francis copied down the hieroglyphics engraved upon a calcite wishing-cup, I find it now, below a stanza from Blake.

Mayest thou spend million of years, thou lover of Thebes, sitting with thy face to the North wind and thy eyes beholding felicity.

He has broken up the lines, as though in an attempt to work them into a poem, but I am certain that he never did so. The words speak too much of optimism and serenity, he could not have committed himself to such truth. He was to quote the sentences often to me in the future, but the stanza from Blake is what startles me now, pointing as it does back to the mood which must have been overtaking him that weekend of snow and in which, so greatly accentuated, I again found him.

Like a fiend in a cloud
With howling woe
After night I do croud
And with night will go.
I turn my back on the East
From whence comforts have increas'd
For light doth seize my brain
With frantic pain.

He did not come to lunch with me. I thought that I should
go and find him. It seemed most urgent that I should do so. I
was unused to acting upon impulse. I went to Paddington
station by taxi. It was one of those freakish days of winter
when the sun shines with a false promise of spring. I sat in the
Oxford train with the reflected warmth of it full on my face.

*

I see every detail of that house in my mind, the uneven
arrangement of the bricks and the way the window-ledges were
sunken in the middle, as though under the press of some heavy
weight.

The sun was shining still but it was bitterly cold, the wind
came howling down all the alleyways and I wore no overcoat.
I felt unreal walking through the streets, unable to believe that
I had come here. The house was in the lower part of the town,
in a mean, dank street, and I found it with some difficulty. It
was not what I knew of Oxford, yet Francis was already known
as a poet and he was not poor.

The curtains hung heavy at the windows, grass grew out of
cracks between the grey roof-slates. I rang the bell and knocked.
No one answered. I went in. Stairs led off to the right but it was
quite dark and I could not find any light switch. The hallway
smelled sour. If I close my eyes now, I am standing there on
the cracked black and white tiles of the floor.

Then I went further, groping about from door to door, and
up two flights of stairs until I found him.

Both the curtains and the blinds of his sitting-room were
tightly drawn, no thread of daylight could get through them.
He was sitting in an armchair and there was an old-fashioned

lantern torch beside him. The bulb had almost gone out and the light came and went, a dim blue-yellow. The fire was banked high with coal and logs and smoking hard, a great billow of it came out into the room as I opened the door.

'Francis ...'

He scarcely glanced up. And then I felt uncertain, I felt foolish, if he had asked me to explain why I had come I could not have done so. But he said nothing and, after a moment, I went into the room. I dreamed about it often later, saw the faint glow from the fire, and his figure, hunched down in the big chair and in the dream, I was always afraid.

'What's wrong?'

He looked up. He had taken off his spectacles and it was as though I were seeing his face as it really was for the first time. He looked much younger and he was very pale. There was a blank expression in his eyes, the planes of his cheekbones and nose were sunken, shadowy.

'Are you ill? I can't see you properly in this torch-light.' I went towards the window.

'*Leave those curtains alone.*' He sprang up from the chair. 'I won't have the daylight in here, I can't stand the daylight.'

'Yes, but ...'

'I WON'T HAVE IT.'

The sound of his suddenly-raised, panic-stricken voice boomed on in the room. He had taken a step towards me.

'All right. But the torch is almost out.'

'Let it go out. I want it to go out.'

'Isn't there a lamp?'

He hesitated. Then sat down again heavily, sinking into the chair as though he were trying to crawl inside himself, to make himself smaller.

'There's a lamp over there, on the bookcase – if you must *see*.'

'Is there something wrong with your eyes?'

'No.'

'You've got a headache?'

'No.'

He volunteered nothing. His voice was remote, unfriendly. I thought he would have preferred it if I had not come.

24

'I was – rather worried that you didn't turn up, that's all.'
'Turn up?'
'For lunch. We were going to have lunch together.'
There was silence for a moment. Then he sighed, shifting a little, to slump down further in the chair. He said, 'Were we? I'm sorry.'
I was still standing. 'Is there anything I can get for you?'
'No.'
'Francis do you need a doctor? There's obviously something wrong with you.'
He began, quite abruptly, to cry, he beat his head against the back of the chair and sobbed, the tears spurting out of his eyes and running down his face, and he made no gesture to rub them away. I had never seen a man cry. I was shocked, and afraid, too, afraid not for him but of him. I stared blankly at his distress, wondering what I had come to, and why.
Then the torch went out. I was very hot in that small room and I felt, rather than saw, the heavy furniture which crowded us in. I had no idea what I should say, or what he expected me to do. But I wanted to get away from him and from the stifling darkness. If I had done so, I should never have gone back, never seen Francis again, and what would have become of him then, how would he have lived?
He stopped crying as suddenly as he had begun and then bent his head, and rubbed his face over and over again on his sleeve. He was wearing a dressing-gown.
'Francis ...'
'You should go.'
'I don't think so.'
'It makes no difference.'
'You can't possibly be left in this state.'
He laughed shortly. 'I generally am.' And then he leaned forward, I saw his eyes gleam in the faint firelight. He began talking, very rapidly.
'Listen, Harvey. Listen, this is what it's like this ... Oh God, I'll tell you, this is how it always happens, and I cannot stop it once it has begun, I know where it's going but I don't know where it will end because each time it gets worse, it terrifies me. Listen, last year I was at home, I went to see my family, to

Scotland, I told you, you know all about them.' (He had told me nothing, never mentioned his family to me.)

'It was in the summer, it was hot and I couldn't bear it, the sun was so *bright* – I kept on trying to get away from it. If I can just get away, you see, like this, in the darkness, it's better. Then I did try but ... it's not so easy when you're living in ... when there are other people. They don't trust me at home now, something happened once before and ... But I tried. Then I began to be afraid, I was afraid of everything, of the thoughts in my head – it makes me sweat, I couldn't ... I walk about, you know, you've been with me, I wake at night, I dare not go to sleep. And they found out, it had happened before and I said that I was better, it was all right, but I couldn't go to sleep, they found me ... I told them. Listen, what do you do when you are most afraid, what do you *do*? I couldn't get away from it, I wanted to climb out of my head and I did what ... I went to my mother. It was all I could think of. I told my mother. I felt ... and then the next day I heard her, she was telling them, she was talking about me, *they* were talking about me, I heard them through the door of the drawing-room, she said, "There's something wrong with him again. He ought to go away. I said that before. He needs treatment. *We ought to send him away*."'

He stopped and there was silence in the room. When he spoke again, his voice was unsteady, with grief or rage. He said, 'I can never go there again, I shall never dare to go there again.'

That was the beginning, then, of one of his worst fears, that he would be sent away, that any one of us might betray him, and would send secretly for doctors, have him committed to what he often called 'a place' – an asylum. There were times when he dreaded going out with me in any unfamiliar streets, he was so afraid of where I might be leading him. I think he trusted me as much as he could trust anyone, yet until his death the old suspicion, the deepest fear, never left him. There was nothing I could do to gain his entire trust. And in the course of time, I did 'betray' him. But I learned never to mention the words 'doctor' or 'treatment', and never to suggest that we go anywhere new. The wish to move on, the restlessness, always came from him. I have wondered whether he was right, whether, after all, he should not have submitted himself, voluntarily and for a long period, to expert medical care in a good hospital. Perhaps it would have worked for him, but after his one terrible experience, he went in dread of the white-coated men.

On that first afternoon, I mentioned the war to him, but he shook himself like a dog, not simply his head but his whole body. 'No, no. That's too easy. It began years ago, it began at school, it has always been there. I had to get out of the daylight – like this. But in France, it never happened, I was perfectly well the whole time I spent there – listen to me, I was bloody terrified, it was war, I saw men killed, every day I saw things I cannot bear to remember, but I was *all right*. It was quite different. I could cope with it. Oh, if it had been the war, it would be easy, I should at least have an excuse shouldn't I? Everyone would accept it. Can't you understand?'

'Yes.' Though I could not altogether, not yet.

'Ah.' He fell back in his chair as though he were completely exhausted.

'A doctor would be able to give you something to calm you down a bit, help you to sleep. Perhaps you need to sleep for a long time.'

'I will not see any doctors.'

'Why not? They ...'

'*NO.*'

It was this that terrified me most, this sudden roar of fury and refusal.

I felt about in the darkness for a chair. I had no idea how long I might have to stay there with him, whether he had other friends, whether anyone at all would come. The closeness of the room was making me dull-headed.

'Why have you come here? You're supposed to be in London.'

'We had a lunch appointment. You didn't arrive.'

'I don't remember.'

'It's all right.'

'I don't always remember things.'

'How long will you want to stay like this – in the dark?'

'I can't bear the daylight. This is better. This is all right for me.'

'And it's happened often before?'

27

'Oh, there are always different things, new things. It gets worse. It changes. Last night, I was trying to remember my own name, I forgot who I was.'

Then I began to be seriously alarmed, even to think about how I might manage to fetch a doctor without his permission, how I might contact some hospital. Oh, if he had known what was in my mind then, how little he could really afford to trust me, if he had realized what a poor risk I was!

'My head hurts, I get a pain right down inside my head.' He was complaining now in the voice of a small child. I was shocked at the total difference in his manner between that first weekend I met him, and the languid, extravagant way he spoke, the way he showed off, the amusement he seemed to keep bottled within himself, and the way he was now, the change simply in his tone of voice.

'Would it help you to have a drink?'

'No.'

I was floundering and appalled by my own helplessness, as I am appalled, looking back upon that day, at the naïvety of my own suggestions, the total uselessness of them all. I understood nothing, I had everything to learn.

'They must not know about me – I mean the people in this house. There is a woman downstairs – the woman with the child. If people know, they want to do the wrong things, they want to put me away.'

'They need not find out.'

'I shall never go home to my family, I shall never dare to take that risk.'

'They must have been anxious for you, that was all. They wanted to do what they thought best.'

'They wanted to ...' he leaned forward again and spoke very quietly, staring intently into my face, 'I'm not *mad*, Harvey. I'm all right, I'm not mad.'

'I know.'

'How can you possibly know? What can you know about it?'

'I know that you are not mad.' Though I did not know. I knew nothing.

'Is that what you believe?'

I said, 'Yes,' and he seemed to accept it.

For a long time then, we sat in silence. The drawn blinds muffled any sounds there might have been in the street outside. I had no more doubts that I had been right to come here. I was no longer afraid of him. When he next spoke, he sounded more like himself, but very tired.

'Really, you should go, you shouldn't stay with me.'

'I think I should.'

'No. You ought to go home.'

'No.'

The fire was beginning to blaze upwards, blood-red at the centre.

'I can't work. I can't do anything. I don't know where it will end.'

'Don't worry about it. Do you have anything in the house to eat?'

'Oh, never mind about that. What we need are candles. I love the light from candles, that's what we should have.'

'Do you want me to go out and buy some?'

'Oh, yes, yes. Some candles.'

I got up and at once, so did Francis, he put his hands on my shoulders and gripped me tightly.

'Don't go *away*.'

'No.'

'You promise me that you'll come back here, you promise me?'

'Yes.'

'With candles?'

'With candles.'

'Not a doctor?'

'No.'

He gave a quick sigh of relief.

When I returned, the room was as hot as a furnace, the flames seemed to be flickering all around the walls and at first I could not see him. Then I heard a slight sound. He was kneeling on the floor in the centre of the room, with his hands up, fingers feeling the bones of his cheek and jaw. He started and looked up at me, his eyes enormous, dark, and his skin glowing dull orange in the firelight. I saw that he was weeping again, and when he spoke, his voice was thick with fear. He said, 'I can't get it off, it won't come off, I can't get it away.'

'What is it?'

'This isn't my own face but it won't come off, don't you see what's wrong, *it isn't my own face.*' And he began to tear at the skin with his fingers.

•

Saturday

Now I will describe this man Harvey Lawson. His eyes are green, not that cat's green, twig-green which is usual, but grape-green. His eyes are the shape and colour of pale green grapes, his eyes have the full, watery look of grapes, which may possibly burst. I went on looking at his eyes, because I was startled by him, his voice made me jumpy. But I think that he does not like me. He will not be my friend.

It would shock anyone to know that I was truly happy throughout the war. It shocks me. But the truth is the truth. I was never once afraid, and there I always had a friend, I had a friend of a week or a night, a turn of duty, for we were all friends then, the whole Company. And the men were friendly. I could go out any night and talk to them. I loved them. It has never been like that in my life before or since. I have not the knack. School was bad and then Oxford, and perhaps that is why I am still living there, trying to make it open up for me as it did for the others. For there is a pearl in the very centre and that is, success and friends. Yet this woman invited me here, she had scarcely met me, and so it is as easy as that. But was it because she *liked* me? Ah.

Saturday night

I liked best that he told me he did not read any poetry, which meant mine, I suppose. But I pretended to mind. One should mind. Oh, I do not, I have found that there is admiration, adulation and people will come around me, chattering like birds, eating out of my hand because of the books lettered with my name, and I had so many hopes of all of them, I was excited each day by the people and the letters they wrote, I thought I had discovered the secret at last. But that is not friendship. I am thirty-three years old and I have been so long in discovering the truths which even children know.

Yet when I was a child, I did know them.

Godmother Bennett sent me a fat, fruity iced cake, in a special tin, the tin had a great, puce rose embossed upon the lid, and I gave it all away, every piece, cutting them quite small so that very many boys might have some and there would be very many chances of making a friend. They all came round me and ate, and I felt it to be very painful, watching the cake disappear into their red mouths. But it was gone and then they were gone too, and nothing had changed after all.

Why do I remember this when it is nothing, nothing? For I am a lucky man, I think, I am fortunate, if there is such a thing as fortune.

I loved cake, I loved sweet things, I love sweet slabs of chocolate. I wish I were in Vienna now, eating layered torte, with cream and coffee. Vienna is best for the river and the coffee and cake.

But I have always work to do, there are so many things to taste and see, to think about and speak about, and that is what matters, and so I am not lonely, I am very self-supportive, very full of chances.

Sunday

I should like to have him for a friend. I am afraid of being alone when I am ill (because it will always come back). If nobody knows about it, then there will be nobody to stand between me and the world, and the world will send doctors and priests in long, long skirts and I shall be put in a very small room somewhere, with a high window and a bed and no carpet and a spy hole in the door.

There seems to be no reason at all why I should have found this one person today, rather than another. Or else there is every reason. Things make a pattern.

He is not so tall as I am, and his body is made quite differently, he is thick, there is more of him packed between front bones and backbone. He has rather short arms. He stands all of a piece, as though he were sending roots down into the ground. His head is very square, a very solid skull. I see that if I battered him with a wooden plank and rammed him with a wooden pole, he would not budge. I should not be able to fracture him. He is not a polyp, as I am. I feel every day as if I shall burst open and spew out anyhow from the bag of my skin and leave only bone. I am all bones and bones break. I think of myself lying in my tomb, a pile of bones.

I wake up and it has begun again, the blood is squeezing hard through my head. I have to stand holding on to the wall. I dare not move away from it.

I went to find H. and we walked out into the snow and then it was better, I could breathe and I wanted to roll myself in great wads of snow. I asked him to come and he came. I was afraid he would hit me. But it is *all right*. Perhaps.

The owl which came through the wood had a mask for a face, its eyes were like lights shining through the holes. I should have screamed at it. I thought of its beak and claws and the death of something, a mouse or a vole, the soft body pierced open and blood spattered on to the snow.

> Hinweg ists, und die Erd' ist kalt,
> Und der Vogel der Nacht schwirrt
> Unbequem vor das Auge dir.

H. told me a proverb. 'I have lived too near a wood to be afraid of owls.'

I think that I should leave Oxford. I always want to go, to be somewhere else. I dream about it, only that it is never what I want when I arrive. So I should live near a wood and perhaps I would never be ill again. Or I shall go to a place in the sun where people stroll up and down in cool clothes, arm in arm, and smile up into one another's face and do not fear anything or quarrel because of this warmth and loving-kindness from the rays of the sun. I should be well there, I could swim and I should be well.

Tuesday

There are only four poems written and now Fowlers want more for a new volume, they keep writing to me, but nice letters, affable letters, they call me Dear Francis and want to know how I am, and that is kind of them, I should be grateful for such kindness. I want to write a long poem, a very long – perhaps, I mean, half a book or more. It will be difficult. And now there is the owl poem, but that is only short.

Another proverb is, 'The owl does not praise the light nor the wolf the dog.'

Wednesday

I have re-written the owl poem.

Masks and faces. But I cannot begin yet.

Well, we should go to the sea. I say 'we' ... We shall find Punch and Judy there and that is the cruellest story. At the seaside you see the most wonderful things. Men with their faces painted black and white, singing and dancing. I shall buy paint and make a new face for myself. If I were a woman I could paint my eyelids green and my mouth as red as a pomegranate, but why not the other way about?

If we went to Brighton or some such place, we could look into the machines where there are little wax dolls acting a tableau, the woman taking off her clothes and the condemned prisoner, going to be hanged and then hanged by the neck till he be dead. For only a penny.

I dreamed of lying down and being first snuffled over and then eaten by a cow, chewed around and round in the cow's huge wet mouth, for it would not swallow whole, like Jonah's whale. 'All flesh is grass.'

Thursday

But I did not ask him if he would come with me and probably he will not want to go anywhere. He sits at a desk in the British Museum or potters about among cases and cabinets writing and reading those strange picture languages about Isis and Osiris and the bird of folly and the bird of knowledge. It is a marvellous world, and so he may not come with me.

Friday

I will live on fruit, nothing but fruit forever. I ate four oranges at once, I love the feel of the pulp as I bite.

I read a poem I wrote at school, I think just before the first time I was ill. We had been dissecting rats. I can remember the formaldehyde, the dreadful smell. But the poem says that I enjoyed it. I was excited, it says, that was the truth. How *can* that be? But it is more than fifteen years ago, I am not the same person.

Then I am afraid that this person I am now and know myself to be will be betrayed utterly by some future self, of whom I as yet know nothing. And I do not know myself at all when I am ill and what might I do then to betray myself? I feel my own self slithering through my fingers like blood. There are masks like layers of skin and until we peel off the first layer we cannot know the next and when we are wearing the next to the world, we have forgotten and betrayed the one which went before. And can you ever stop still, can you shout No, and stay the same, keep the same face forever, now and forever?

But I am older, I am thirty-three, perhaps I shall change less.

H. is thirty-four. He writes that he will take me to the Museum and show me mummies and death masks and beautiful statues of gold.

I cannot go out. I am writing this in the darkness. I cannot go out.

Monday

There are forests inside my head, where owls sit, laughing, laughing, laughing. I want ...

*

'Do you play the piano? Yes, yes, play it, let's have a noise. I want a noise.'

'No – I took lessons until I was ten or so, the way we all do. Nothing since. I was no good at it.'

'Let me look at your hands, Harvey, show me your hands, come on, put them on the table, spread them out, come on.'

I did as he asked. It seemed best to follow up his whims when I could. Just as it seemed best to answer all his questions no matter how distracted or apparently nonsensical. I think it calmed him a little, just to have me speak to him in a normal voice. Certainly, he would listen, his eyes watching the movements of my mouth intently as though he were lip-reading. So long as I spoke he was silent. I think he paid more attention to the tone of my voice than to what I said, it seemed to reassure him. His own voice was still quite changed, he spat or shouted out questions and comments, his throat sounded tight and strained, as though he were always just on the point of bursting into tears.

We were still sitting by candlelight, which was all that he could bear and we kept the fire banked high. Once I went out to buy food, and once, a newspaper and a copy of Ruskin's *The Stones of Venice*, both of which he demanded as urgently as if his life entirely depended upon them, and then ignored as soon as I brought them in. Indeed, he burned the paper, twisting the sheets up into spills.

The night had passed somehow, I had slept for perhaps a couple of hours, uneasily, on the sofa. Francis had sung to me, in a high, tuneless voice and it was scarcely a melody, only a line of sound which rose and fell arbitrarily and which, after a while, I found oddly soothing, like some Tibetan chant. I do not think that he slept at all. Once, just as I was at the brink of sleep, he knelt down by my side, his face close to mine.

'Don't be *afraid* of me. I shan't harm you: Don't be afraid.'

I told him that I was not, and it was the truth, all my alarm had left me hours before.

I had been here now for almost two days, during which he became more and more agitated and distressed in bouts: at times he was quite incoherent, half-mumbling, half-crying, like a spastic child. But, in between, he became lucid, he lay back in the armchair, pale and exhausted as if he had run a race, his eyes closed. He said that the bats had left his brain. When he spoke then, his voice was a little slurred, he could scarcely summon up enough to breathe in and out and form the syllables.

I had no idea how long I should have to stay, when or how it might end. The thought that I should send for a doctor came back repeatedly to my mind. But I knew he would not allow it, and that I should betray him utterly if I called one against his wishes.

His main fear, immediately, seemed to be that the landlady, who lived below, might find out about his illness and ask him to leave. She had, he said, noticed once before that he was behaving strangely, locking himself away. Francis swore that he could not bear to leave this house, that he was attached to it, he would never be comfortable and secure in any other rooms. I could not understand him. The place was dingy, stuffy, cramped, the street was poor and out of the way. There seemed no good reason why he had chosen to live here. I went out and telephoned to the Museum, made some excuse about my absence. I neither knew nor cared whether it would matter. Francis could not be left. In three days, he had become more important than my work. That was fascinating, it absorbed me – I suppose I would have said that I 'could not bear to be parted from it'. But I had left it, and it now seemed remote and uninteresting, my deciphering of ancient hieroglyphics, the delving into the past of a remote civilization – I did not see that it was of any value to me at all except as a way of passing the time.

One half of me was shocked that this should be so. I wanted to refuse the change Francis and his illness had so abruptly brought about in me. Why should I care, and was I even doing the right thing in staying alone with him in this darkened room? Had I not a plain duty to get him proper care?

'*They will send me away.*'

I understood the terror in his mind, the thought of locked doors and demented sounds echoing from other rooms, the probing questions. If he went into an asylum he felt certain that he would finally lose his grip on what remained of himself, that he would never be fully well again. He said, 'It always goes, in the end.' I believed him, though I wondered, as his enormous, pale eyes stared at me, for how long this would be so, and whether one day he might not tip over the precipice of madness and fail ever afterwards to find a foothold, to scramble back.

My hands were spread out flat upon the table, the candlelight making them look yellowish and waxen. Francis leaned over them, he felt down each finger, then laid his whole hand on top of mine. His fingers were very long and bony, the nails beautifully shaped.

He shook his head. 'No, no, it won't do, my dear, it will never do at all, don't you see? How *could* you play the piano?'

'I have told you, I cannot.'

He seemed not to have heard me. 'You see, they're so thick and heavy, your fingers are so broad, they ... but you won't listen, you won't be told.' He lifted his hand away. 'I want to have some music. I want to hear the piano. Did you know I had a piano?'

'I'm sorry. I wish I could play.'

'Oh, but I'll show you, I'll play for you, it's so beautiful – listen.'

There was an upright piano in the darkest corner of the room and he took two of the candles across and fitted them carefully into the old, iron brackets which stuck out on either side of the ebony front. He said again, 'Listen', and his face gleamed with a sort of voluptuous anticipation as he leaned over the keys.

The piano was quite out of tune and some of the notes were missing altogether. It scarcely mattered. Whether Francis had ever been able to play, whether what he played sounded like music in his head, I did not know. Certainly, when he was well, he knew and enjoyed a good deal, particularly wind music and opera, and the sound of flute or oboe would often soothe him in the early, restless stages of his madness.

Now, he simply hit his hands down on to the keys, playing as a two-year-old child will play, crashing a dozen notes down at once, delighting in the discordances, yet all the time pretending to 'be a pianist'. I thought of the landlady and her child in the rooms below us.

The music changed, he bent even more closely to the keyboard and began to strike notes softly, one after another, in a chromatic scale, up and down, up and down. I looked at the back of his head, where the thick hair splayed out over his dressing-gown collar. I wanted to weep for him. He played like that for over an hour. When he stopped, he was swaying on the music stool, I got up and caught him as he fell heavily against me. I had to half-drag, half-carry him to the chair. Then, for the first time since I arrived, he slept, a deeply silent, utterly still figure, lying like a fallen, broken, awkward bird, and I sat opposite, watching him.

*

My dear family,

You ask what I am doing, why I have not written and I tell

37

you that for an hour I have played the piano. I have a friend with me. You didn't know that I had a friend. But I shall not tell you his name, I will tell you nothing about him, for fear you take him from me. But he cooks meals for me, bacon and eggs and grilled fish, I would eat nothing but oranges if it were not for him, and if I am what I eat, I should become sharp-sweet and segmented.

But you, brother Andrew, who shoot down birds, you will become feathers and mortal flesh, and they say the Devil is a gamekeeper. There is a particular sphere of hell, which is the outer circle, which is molten lead-shot, and this is for those of you who go through this world hiding behind a gun.

We are very grand, very handsome here, there are tapestried curtains embroidered with the beautiful painted faces of women in gold and silver and an owl on the chimney breast. I have bowls of scented water for my hands and feet. Do you all kneel in a line on Sundays praying for me and all sinners? Then I shall pray for you.

I have this man who is a true friend. He has read the Bible to me, the rejoicing psalm. 'He casts forth his ice like morsels; who can stand before his cold?'

I shall soon go away to live in a wood for the world likes to have night-owls, that it may have matter for wonder, and if it is winter with you in your North country, look carefully at the six-cornered snowflake, and give thanks for that.

I send you greetings and goodwill, for I cannot love you.

*

'Read to me.'

'What shall I read now?'

'Harvey, I won't be a poet any longer, poets are done for, I shall burn all my poems.'

'Don't do that.'

'But I want to write poems. Not thundering poems, not that prose of the giants, not Tolstoy. I have a quiet mind, haven't I? Well, I shall write like Turgenev. Do you know Turgenev?'

'I read a little – *Virgin Soil*.'

'Ah, but what you must know is *Fathers and Sons*.'

Suddenly, he jumped up, went to the window and drew back

38

the curtains, so that only the blind was still down, and a murky, smoky daylight spread into the room. I was startled. When Francis turned back to me his face was shining, triumphant. He said, 'You *see?*'

'Yes.'

'But we will stay like this for now, this is comfortable.'

'Whatever you want.'

He looked deplorable. His hair stood up on end and he had not shaved for three or four days, his beard grew like an uneven stain around his cheeks and jaw, his eyes were bloodshot. The old, faded tartan dressing-gown was held up anyhow with a belt that did not belong to it.

Having a little light in the room made it look infinitely worse. There was an enormous, dark oak table and sideboard, the chairs were mud-coloured leathercloth, books were piled everywhere, all over the piano top and floors and table. The fire was almost out, the grate heaped with pale, dirty ash. There was candle-grease lying about in pools. I wanted to pull up the blind and open all the windows, to sweep and clean and set things to rights. I was always a tidy man, too tidy. Francis said he told me that it boded no good.

He was rummaging about in a corner among the books. Behind him, a door led to his bedroom and bathroom. I had been into them but seen little, except a large, unmade bed, for the curtains were tightly drawn in here too. There was a frowsty smell just as, in the sitting-room, the air was stale with the smoke and candle fumes and the breathing of three days and nights. Two trays with the remains of our meals and half a dozen mugs and glasses were piled up on the sideboard.

But if Francis looked better, he was by no means well again, he could not yet bear the full light, and when he talked he was still excited and intermittently incoherent, his face was pale and then flushed. I dared not try to rush him forwards, and I was still largely ignorant about the nature and course of his illness, for all I knew this might be only a break before a worse darkness came upon him again.

'I have it, it's here.' He bounced across the room with a book in his hand. The cover hung off and the pages were loose. 'This is what I want.' It was *Fathers and Sons*.

'Read it to me, Harvey.'

'From the beginning?'

'Can you?'

'Yes, of course, but ...'

'What is it? What's the matter? Why won't you help me?'

He was fidgeting his hands, rolling thumbs and forefingers together in agitation, he looked as if he might burst into tears of frustration.

'It's nothing. Sit down.'

'You want to go, don't you? You're not going to stay with me.'

'Of course I shall stay.'

He closed his eyes and I saw that now his hands were trembling.

'Sit down again. Everything is all right.'

I had been only going to suggest that I tidy up a little before I began reading to him. I felt I could not bear the squalor of it all a moment longer. I was worn out, my limbs were cramped, there was a stale taste in my mouth. But I saw that he would not be able to put up with any disturbance at all. He was sitting with his back to the window. 'Read to me.'

I read. He listened in silence, like a small child, his eyes on my face. I read for over an hour, without a pause, then made a pot of coffee in his tiny kitchen before returning to read again. It was nearly evening when I got to the death of Bazarov. The light was beginning to fade to a sepia tint through the drawn blinds. My head was pounding.

'There's strength enough,' he muttered. 'It's all there still and yet I must die ... An old man at least has had time to become disenchanted with life but I ... Yes, just try and set death aside. It sets you aside and that's the end of it. So it turns out there was no point in thinking about the future. Death is an old jest but it comes new to everyone. Russia needs me ... No, clearly she does not ... And who is needed? The cobbler's needed, the tailor's needed, the butcher sells meat, the butcher ...'

I read to the end of the book. It had moved me greatly, in spite of the exhaustion of reading it all aloud in the space of a few hours. But when I looked at Francis, I was alarmed by the change that had come over his features. He was not pale, so much as grey, his eyes were glazed and his mouth peculiarly twisted – for a moment, I wondered if he had had some kind of physical stroke. Then he said, in a deadened voice, 'That's the truth about it, isn't it? That's what I should have learned. There is no point in my being here, Harvey, because *I am not needed*. Who is needed? "The cobbler's needed, the tailor's needed, the butcher sells meat ..." '

I saw that it was pointless to begin any reasoned arguments about the value of poetry and the worth of the poet, or even about the value of his life simply as a human being. He could not accept any of it, and I understood why, for I had seen when I first arrived here that there was no innate value in my own work, that I was 'not needed'.

Oh, now I know that that is not true, even of me, and perhaps at heart I knew it then. Certainly I believed that Francis was needed, as a man and as a poet. He had become necessary to me. But a kind of despair filled us. I was infected with the sense he had received from Turgenev about his own worthlessness.

But I think now that if I had not been so overwhelmed by his mood, if he had not influenced me so entirely then, that I should have been of no use to him in the future. It was because I had glimpsed into the heart of his despair, because I had shared it a little, though only temporarily, that I understood why I must stay with him not only now but for as long as he might need me in the future.

That night, for the first time since my arrival, he felt calm enough to sleep in the bedroom. But in the middle of an uneasy night, I heard a sound and woke at once, to find Francis kneeling beside me on the floor.

'What is it?'

He said quietly, 'I shall die. I shall breathe once and then never again and then I shall go down to hell. I have to die and there is nothing I can do or you can do to keep me from it.'

Nor was there anything I could say to him, because it was the truth and I would offer no spurious comfort. What he said about hell he believed, then and always, he had a conviction that in the end he would be overtaken by the devil, though there were times when he also felt absorbed by God and goodness. That sense of the holiness of all life except his own pervades the poems of his last years.

'I have to die.' He was shaking. I put my arms around him and said nothing, and in the end, still kneeling, he went to sleep.

*

Harvey,

Now I begin and do not know what to say. The sun is shining into the room, right into my face. I love the sun, I love all bright, shining, glittering things.

I have been afraid to write to you. I have been out all this morning, walking beside the river. I am afraid of what you will say to me.

Harvey, I must go away. I cannot be here any longer. I must work and that I cannot do in Oxford. I *must* go away.

Perhaps we should go to the South of France, and walk along those smart, deserted promenades and I could sit out on a balcony in my overcoat and work. But you would perhaps not like it there, the people who stay for the winter are old, wrinkled, musty people. You would not be happy. But I must work. So I shall go away. So now I am asking you to come with me. I dare not be by myself. But that is not all, not all ... Perhaps we should go to a Spa? The waters might be good for me. I read about a man called Dr Wittie, who wrote in 1660, to recommend Spa waters 'for the drying up of superfluous humours and preserving from putrefaction'.

Oh, that is marvellous, that is what I need. Preservation from putrefaction. I look down on my arms and I love that flesh, that flesh is mine, is of me, and how can I bear it to rot?

Shall we go away?

I have burned all the candles now, there is a religious smell.

I have written three longish poems in two days and I am very tired but my head is spinning with ideas, and *I am well*, and I shall make a little money, it will not cost us a great deal to go away.

There are days when I would do anything to leave this place.

Now here I shall write down for you something entirely good and simple, and this is how I wish I were able to write.

And would you see my mistress' face?
It is a flowery garden place
Where knots of beauties have such grace
That all is work and nowhere space.

That is Thomas Campion and I shall never do anything half so good. We all think such clotted thoughts, we all tangle up our words.

Now write me a postcard and say where we shall go.

*

We went to the sea. Though not to a Spa; in the end he felt there would be too many old, sick, suffering faces there, he did not want to be among invalids, for he was in that vulnerable, delicate state immediately after recovery when he could not bear to be reminded that he had been ill. He wanted change, he wanted to look forward, he was always so hopeful.

Besides, he said that he would not like the 'insipid grace of the eighteenth century', which is how he saw all those elegant, white-stuccoed Spa towns.

We went to the East coast, to a small plain fishing town whose edge reached down almost into the North sea. Francis could not bear to stay in a hotel, and so I managed to rent a small house for us at the quiet end of the foreshore. It was February.

He told me that he had not for a moment expected me to go with him, though he dreaded hearing me say so, he waited for the post each day sick with apprehension. But there had never been any question in my mind, not as to what I ought to do, what might be dutiful, but what I wanted. I wanted to be with Francis. I had never known anyone like him. It was not a question of accepting his dependence upon me, for he was well now and might be well for months. It was not that.

I thought at first of taking a month's holiday from the Museum. Then I knew that would not serve. I handed in my resignation. I could still work if I chose to, while I was away with Francis, I could begin a monograph I had planned on the nomenclature of the fifth dynasty Pharaohs. Or I could not, I could read and enjoy the world. That seemed to be more important.

Like Francis, I was not poor, though my father had begun so. It was my mother, who died on Armistice Day, in 1918, who had left me an income which would keep me in comfort, though not in luxury. How lucky we were, for if we had both been poor men, if I had been obliged to work for my living, we could not have gone away as we did.

And now, getting away had become essential. Francis sent me a long telegram, saying that his landlady had asked him to leave, because of the noise he made and because she found him unreliable. Remembering the piano playing, I was scarcely surprised, and could not blame her. I expected him to be upset, but he was angry, he roared at me that he had been bitterly insulted, that he cursed all such people.

He came to stay with me in London for a few days until we left for Suffolk and it was then that he began the long poem called 'Janus', which is perhaps his best work, though it is difficult and, sometimes, I prefer the shorter, more lyrical poems. Others have praised the second long poem as being more mature. But 'Janus' influenced a whole school of later poets, it is this poem which all the learned critics study.

He wrote it very quickly to begin with, sitting at my dining-room table in Sackville Street, with a glass of Apollinaris water at his elbow. It was all the later stanzas which took so long, which seemed to defeat him day after day during those six weeks we spent by the sea. He would walk along the beach and across the marshes alone for hours, talking to himself, revising the lines in his head and then come back to write, alter, re-write painstakingly: the first manuscript of 'Janus' has scarcely a word left as it was originally written. He talked to me about it very little, but the problem did not seem to be that he did not know what he was trying to say: it was there, packing his mind, but he felt inadequate to express it all, the words, he said, were never good enough.

But there is much more I remember about that time, that end-of-winter, beginning-of-spring, and I remember it in so much detail because I have come back to live only a mile or so out of the town, my house is on the edge of the marshes across which Francis walked towards the sea. While I could still walk myself, I followed the same paths almost every day. The colour of the sky, the silver-blue, steely reflection off the face of the sea, the faint, dry, keening wind blowing across the flat land, all this links my present, the life I have lived here alone, with the past, some of my time with Francis, so that I feel there is no past, nothing is dead, for nothing has changed, there is only a mirror into which I look and see at once what is now and what was then.

I cannot go far now, I am ungainly as a stork upon my two sticks. I can only listen to the sifting of the sea, and lick my dry lips to taste the salt which is on the air, I can sit here in my garden and watch the changing sky. It is a beautiful place.

*

We arrived after dark and walked from the railway station, downhill through the quiet cold streets leading to the sea. As we came within sight of it, Francis gripped my arm for a second, I saw his exulting face, the gleaming bones, and then he began to run, out from between the last of the huddled houses, and across the cobbles to where the shingle began. I lost sight of him, only heard his footsteps crunching away from me. I was filled with relief, to see him so much better, to know that we had done the right thing in coming here.

It was a very calm sea and then the moon came riding gracefully out from behind the clouds and sent a shiver of light across the glistening surface. I saw Francis's tall figure standing right down at the edge of the water. I heard him laughing to himself.

When I was beside him, he said, 'Oh, there are things the world never dreams of.' He seemed overjoyed and yet quite tranquil, quite settled within himself.

'This is good, this is what I want, I shall be able to work now.'

'I'm glad.'

'All those days and nights there were bats clinging to the walls of my head. I couldn't shake them off. They only beat their wings sometimes. But then they were gone. They always do go. I'm better than I have ever been.'

He smiled. 'I don't make any sense, my dear, really I oughtn't to bore you so!'

For the first time, he sounded like himself again – or rather, like the man I had originally met, for which was Francis's true self?

He put his arm across my shoulders as we walked slowly along looking for the house. The moon came and went, and there was only the crisp sound of our footsteps. I think that I was entirely happy that night, as full of joy as I was ever to be.

Our sitting-room was on the first floor, overlooking the water, and there Francis went on with 'Janus', getting up at dawn every morning and basking in the rising sun which rippled across the sea and shone so warmly through the window, though outside there was a fine silver frost on the shingle and the air took my breath away, thin and cold as a mountain top.

Those days were very peaceful. I hired an elderly bicycle with a basket on the front and went off shopping, to roars of glee from Francis, I looked so unbalanced, he said, 'like a bulldog on a pin'. I cooked for us, though monotonously and not well. What he liked best was to wait until the afternoon, when the fishermen's boats came bounding home across the waves and the slippery fish poured out of their baskets, and then he would go down, striding like a crane over the beach, often in the old carpet slippers he could not be bothered to change, so that his feet were bruised on the shingle, he had to pick his way back fastidiously as a cat with his parcel of fish, which always tasted too coarse and strong.

But once, he returned empty-handed, his face shadowed over. It was a lowering, blustery day. He came into the room, where I was reading Stendhal by the fire. His hands were trembling.

'It's nothing,' he said quickly, 'it's nothing. I'm so stupid.'

'What happened?'

'I must not, I must not be ... Harvey, I'm well now, aren't I, tell me I'm well.'

'Of course you are.'

'Tell me I shall stay so.'

'I think so.'

'Listen, I had to come back, I couldn't stay down there. I was waiting by the hut, the men were bringing up the fish – they were strewn about and shining and dead, they had blood on their mouths.'

'But you've seen that every day, it's always the same.'

'No, no, I've never seen this. Lying on the slab, you know, where they gut the fish when you buy it, there was' one whole cod by itself, a large one. The man had his back to me, sharpening his knife, and I stood waiting, I was looking at that fish, it was *dead* but when the wind blew and it blew into the fish through its open mouth, the gills fluttered – they rose and fell, rose and fell, it was breathing, it was alive. But it was dead. The wind kept on puffing into it like bellows. I couldn't stay there and look at it.'

It was at times like this that I felt most helpless, for there was nothing to say. It was a gruesome, trivial moment, it would have given me a frisson, perhaps, but more probably, I should not even have noticed the fish. But it was precisely the kind of incident which could tip Francis's mind momentarily over into terror and confusion. It was not a question of his being, as my mother would have put it, 'nervy'. His nightmares were dark, blood-filled, they galloped away with him, and he had hallucinations sometimes during the day, even now, when he was well, they filled him with panic. He was reading de Quincey and I was half-afraid that he might try to find some refuge in opiates himself. But I think he knew that they would only accentuate the worst symptoms of his illness, that he would suffer from far more horrifying visions than the fever his own brain generated. He had a suspicion, of all palliatives, he would even go on suffering from quite severe pain from a headache or neuralgia, rather than take aspirin.

The image of the dead, yet breathing fish remained in his mind for days, he would look down at his paper or out to sea, and it was there before his eyes, he would raise his hand to try and brush it away. But his work was absorbing him, he knew that, however slowly he might be writing, he was writing well.

There were days when the estuary on the far side of the marshes lay still and bright as a sheet of metal under the sun and the reeds threw fine, straight shadows on to the water. There were days when the clouds hung low and there was mist like a sweat, the air smelled close and foetid, and we walked slowly, as though unable to breathe, we waited for something to happen. The mallards skimmed very low, their wings creaking together, we heard the eerie, chromatic laugh of the curlew. The colour was bleached out of shingle and sky, reed beds and sea. Gulls dived and hovered and occasionally rose up in a flock, to burst in mid-air like a shower of confetti.

Often, Francis wanted to walk alone, and what he preferred were the stormy days, when a gale whipped up the sea, the breakers came racing in, curd-white along their crests, and the rain drummed into his face. I watched him from the window, pushing himself forwards against the wind, bending in it like a sapling. He was exhilarated, his skin flushed then, and when he came in, he sat down at once to work, the pen scratching in that awkward, oriental writing, which crossed the white page like a line of bird-prints in snow.

He had hideous dreams, when the faces of beasts and birds of prey leered over him, their mouths snarling open and emitting a queer, phosphorous light, and sometimes he dreamed that he was dancing, a ferocious, demonic reel, his feet took over and carried him away and he dared not try to stop, for if he did so he would instantly become paralysed, frozen in mid-position like a run-down clockwork toy, he would never be able to move again.

But in fact I am putting together what he told me in spasms, months, even years afterwards, for he never recounted his nightmares at the time, fearing that to do so would embed them even more firmly in his mind.

It was one of the clear, sunlit, springlike days that he chose to tell me what he most dreaded.

It was early afternoon and we had strolled along the beach, close to the water's edge. The tide was out, the water a jewel-like translucent blue, the pebbles were rose-pink and marble-white. Our footsteps sucked into the smooth, watery sand and left ridge marks.

'I want to sit down here,' Francis said, and began to arrange the pebbles for me, with a great show of concern, telling me to make sure I had my coat tucked underneath me, in case of seeping damp. He began to pick up flat stones and send them spinning over the water, where they bounced and skimmed and bounced again. It was a trick I admired and could never do, I watched him enviously. There was a fine dexterity in his hands.

'There is something I have to tell you.'

'Yes?'

'And when I tell you, you will leave me at once, I shan't blame you. I would leave myself, Harvey, if I could.'

'You know I shall not.'

'You haven't heard this, this is the worst thing.'

'It makes no difference.'

A stone hit the water four times before sinking. He had averted his face from me but now he turned, he scrutinized me as he spoke for any sign of my recoil from him.

'I tried to kill my brother. He is much stronger than I am. If he hadn't been so, I would surely have killed him. But I cannot remember why. They say a violent man forgets.'

'You're not a violent man.'

'But I don't forget how it was, I can tell you every detail of it – but I shan't. I remember what happened. It is only that I can't find any reason for it.'

'You don't like your brother, you've told me that, you hate the way he lives his life, shooting and trapping.'

'That is not sufficient reason to want him dead and to try and kill him myself.'

'No.'

He said coldly, 'Shall you go now?'

'No.'

'Harvey. You *should* go. You will do no good to stay with me, no good to yourself. You should get out now, while I'm well, while I can manage.'

'No.'

'Well, I have told you, never forget that I have told you.'

'I'm grateful that you did.'

'*They* won't forget, I can tell you that, none of them – that's why they want to put me away, that's why they talk about me as if I'm a leper. I suppose that I am. Only not contagious. Can you blame them for fearing me? They want to have done with it all.'

I got up. I think that I ought to have been frightened by what he told me. I should have been warned. In fact, I was never to think of it again, until he reminded me. But that is later, that is at the end.

I wish that I had a photograph of Francis, for my memory comes and goes now, it flickers over him and will not show me his face. He would never be photographed, he had a terror of the eye of the camera, probing into him, knowing him, setting him down. Yet what would a photograph show me? A dead man, an image, like a butterfly, dried and pinned under a glass, which disintegrates to powder if human breath ever blows upon it. I should not have any more of him by looking at his picture on the desk before me.

Tonight I have closed the notebooks. It gives me too much pain to see his handwriting, which changed so greatly, like his voice, when he was mad : it became erratic, it rose and fell in waves upon the page, and then it was cramped up so small that I can scarcely decipher it. It gives off a smell of madness.

When I have written what I have to write I shall destroy all the papers. Perhaps I shall burn them, perhaps I shall walk for the last time down to the sea and sink them there. For I will not have the bones of them picked over, I will not have those arrogant, salacious young men sniffing about his books like vultures over carrion. And if what I shall do is wrong, I shall bear the burden of it, for I am an old man, I am soon to die. Since i became so helpless, the thought of death has become almost congenial to me, though when I was strong I relished life, I devoured it, for who in his prime can truly wish to die. The flesh is too strong and the spirit fights. Only the cowards and the very brave look for death and I am a commonplace man.

Today there have been more letters, they are pursuing me again.

Mrs Mumford brings me a jar of strawberry jam and I eat it, dipping in a spoon and taking great, dark gobbets into my mouth, the taste is sweet and ripe. I am no longer so fastidious. On some nights I sleep here on the sofa in my clothes, wrapped in a rug, and the gentle, warm air of summer comes to me through the open window. I am as happy as when I slept under the hedges of Southern Italy as a very young man, and woke when there were still stars, fading before the seeping daylight. I remember the smell of the dry grass crushed beneath me, the taste of it against my mouth, I remember the figs bought at dawn from a farmer's wife and eaten, one after another until they were gone, I can feel my teeth biting into the fat, bland flesh. But all that was before I met Francis, when I still had my own future, like an undiscovered city at my feet.

It was insignificant. I would not wish for that time again.

*

Tuesday

If 'Janus' will not come right I am done for and like a fool I have mentioned it to Fowlers and so they will blab about it. I have to pick my way through it so carefully, there is no wool, no wadding. But there are so many things I must say in it, so many truths. Every line is taut, and the lines interlace like wires.

But I am well and this is a marvellous, sea-drenched place, a painter would want to work here, the light is so clear, one can see so far. And going inland there are bracken and gorse and fir trees which interest the eye after so much flat, bright space.

The nights are still bad. I will not think of the nights. Yesterday my eyes felt bruised, swollen, I could not bear the lids to rub against them.

I have written, rather quickly, two short poems, two pieces of mercury, they tripped off the tongue, which is always satisfying, one feels one can get somewhere, do a sprint instead of a long-distance. 'Janus' is so endless, so like untying knot after knot, I must be so *careful* with it. There is appearance and reality, being and seeming, mask and face. I have read *Twelfth Night* again, which is relevant – twins and disguises, mistaken identities. So it has all been said before.

Really a poet ought not to try and write about this place, it would never come off, a painter should paint it, or Turgenev could have described it in a quiet flow of words. It needs to spread, as the sea and sky spread like a watercolour wash, it cannot be cabin'd, cribb'd, confin'd in a poem. Besides, I am not a landscape writer.

The most marvellous thing anyone wrote about a *place* is the first chapter of *The Stones of Venice*.

She is still left for our beholding, in the final period of her decline: a ghost upon the sands of the sea, so weak, so quiet, so bereft of all but her loneliness that we might well doubt, as we watched her faint reflection in the mirage of the lagoon, which was the city and which the shadow.

That's how to do it. Oh, so now we must go to Venice. But not until I have finished 'Janus'. I have no room in me yet for that magnificent decay. When we go, I want to write a set of poems about Venice, a related sequence, all the life I have ever known of there. There is this yearning for another place, always another place. Or the mountains, with the mist like a bonnet. Or I should like to be on a boat going down the Rhine from Mainz to Cologne, past those Cimmerian forests, those toy castles.

Oh, we will go everywhere and that is the answer to my life, I shall travel and drink in so much there will be no time to be ill, no occasion, no *room*.

I have thought of a beautiful picture I should like to own called 'Pegwell Bay', and the pre-Raphaelites will come back into favour with a more discerning generation. H. laughs at me.

In the mornings, the Carroll words run through my head.

'The sun was shining on the sea, shining with all its might,
It did its very best to make the billows smooth and bright,
And this was odd because it was the middle of the night.'

Which is a beautiful sort of madness, if it were like *that* then nothing would matter. Yet they read it to me when I was a child, they read it aloud and thought nothing of it, so why have they turned against me now? They want to send me away. But it is because of Andrew. I tried to kill him. I stare at the words and they are burned into the paper. So I shall have them done in poker-work on a board.

EAST WEST, HOME'S BEST
I TRIED TO KILL MY BROTHER.

I look at H. I look into his face. I cannot tell whether he is afraid of me. He goes down to the sea and plunges into it, he

swims out far across the water and I am terrified for him, his
body looks so small and far away, bobbing, bobbing, like a
bottle, and what is the message inside? He is thick as a tree, his
legs and arms are covered with black hair, it climbs up him like
ivy. He looks as if everything were easy for him, as if he
wrestled and raced and always won. Yet he read Plato and
Ovid and lives among his Egyptians while he cooks the meals,
he is a book-worming man. He swims every day and I gasp for
him as his body hits the water, but he tells me he doesn't feel
the cold. I do not envy him, I only watch him, I love to watch.
I would not know how to manage my body if I were strong.

Friday

There comes a blunt letter from my father, that bigoted, sentimental man, who was gentle as an ox with me, until I grew
up and wrote poetry, and did not become a doctor, as he
planned.

Sunday

'Nothing can happen to any man that nature has not fitted him
to endure.'

I cannot say Amen to that, Aurelius, for what could you
know of the world breaking off bit by bit, brittle as ice in my
hands, and of dreaming that I saw my flesh putrefy and rot and
fall away from my bones as I watched and of the brown,
brackish foaming water that came pouring into my mouth
until I was swollen and bloated as a whale and gushed out of
my broken bag of skin. Nature has not fitted me to that, I must
get out of bed every night and stand at the window to lull
myself with the whispering of the sea. I do not waken Harvey.

Wednesday

'And the new sun rose, bringing the new year.'

Oh, there is nothing, nothing I cannot do. I am drunk with
this power in myself, I go across the silver marshes madly
singing, I have written more than half of 'Janus', I know it will
be all right.

Hemlock: Conium Maculatum. The stem is dull purple, with

a mouse-like smell. The whole plant is smooth with a slight bloom. It is highly poisonous.

Thursday

Somewhere is Atlantis, Avalon, Antilia, St Brendan's Island, the Ile Verte, Lyonnesse and we shall find it, we will go there, and there I shall be well forever and ever. Last night my head felt tight as a drum, I thought it was beginning all over again, but there is God in the power of the lightning flash, who will save me.

But here the sound of the sea rinses through my head, the air is sharp as knives, I can see everything, I shall write all the poetry in the world. Only somewhere outside the door is the Person from Porlock, waiting to knock, waiting to force his way in, and he will say, 'You invited me, I am here as your guest.'

H. has made a beautiful little house of playing cards, balanced upon one another, and inside it is empty air. He is no end pleased with it. He can play solitaire and always end with one marble in the centre. Things are orderly in his mind.

Friday

The world contains exactly five types of regular solid and that is a perfect fact: tetrahedron, cube, octahedron, dodecahedron, icosahedron. That leads me to know the mind of the creator.

Tomorrow we shall walk five miles looking for a heron's nest. H. says ... It is half past eleven, he says, it is bed-time, he says, I dare not go there, I dare not go to sleep. But I do not tell him so.

•

Dear Francis,

Your mother has asked me to write to you because she would find it too upsetting to do so herself upon this delicate subject, which so greatly concerns us and gives us so much anxiety.

It is plain to me from your last letter that you are in a highly nervous and emotional state and you know, as I do, where that may lead. I make some allowances for you because you have shown yourself to be an imaginative man and mental disturbances are, in my opinion, a risk very frequently run by such as yourself.

You have written books which, although I do not profess to understand them, have clearly found favour and critical esteem, and we do not begrudge you that, we are pleased for your success.

But I must advise you, admonish you, to seek professional medical advice and some treatment for that over-wrought condition from which you suffer. You are being unfair not only to yourself but to your family, who care about you, although you say, so cruelly, that you cannot love them. I would ask you to tell us what we have done to forfeit your affection, in what way we are to blame.

I am thankful that you say you have a good, trustworthy friend with you, but a friend is not a blood relation, you are, in the end, putting yourself into the hands of a stranger. It is unfair to him to be obligated to nurse you through some crisis which may suddenly overtake you. I surely do not need to remind you what the consequence of such a crisis may be. You have nothing to fear from the medical profession, you will be treated skilfully, in a place where these matters are understood. It is not a happy thing for me to think that I have fathered a son who may be unbalanced in his mind and who yet stubbornly refuses to accept help for some selfish reason.

Now I have spoken my feelings to you. It was my duty to do so. You are a grown man but you are our son.

Your mother and brother send all blessings.

> Your affectionate father,
> R. P. C. Croft

Francis said, 'I should kill them. Or pray for them.'

*

A week later 'Janus' was finished. He leaned back in the chair one evening, glanced across to where I was sitting with my book, and said, 'That's that.' I could not tell whether he was pleased with it or not. Probably he did not yet know. He came over and put his arms about my neck, he began to laugh, slightly hysterical laughter, his eyes flickering over my face.

He said, 'The owl thinks all her children are beautiful.'

During the next two weeks, he copied out the final version of that long poem, writing very slowly, forming every letter with scrupulous care on sheets of heavy cream paper. The finished manuscript was, simply to look at, a beautiful thing. It gave him such pleasure to work with his hands rather than his brain, he often said he would like to have been an engraver.

It was soothing to watch him as he bent over the table in the window, with the flat, dove-grey sea and sky beyond.

And now they come around me like wasps, asking, asking, wanting to know how it was to be with a great poet all through the time he was writing his best work, and my head fills up, there is so much ... I say, 'I was very happy.' That is all I can tell them. 'I was very happy.'

*

That summer we went to Kerneham, where my godmother had left me a cottage, two miles out of the village, among those dark, prehistoric downs and barrows of north Dorset. I had been there every year since childhood. The villagers knew me, I knew them. Yet we were strangers, for they never took anyone into their midst.

'Janus' had gone to the printer and was to appear on its own : a volume of shorter poems would come out some time later. Francis had exhausted himself. He had come to live in my London flat, where he read ten or a dozen books a week. But for the rest of the time, he began a round of entertainment. He lunched with editors and went to night clubs and smart parties in Hyde Park Gate, he became a little foppish in his dress. I watched him uneasily, not certain that I liked this new, artificial mask he was wearing to the world. He came in very late at night, slept late in the mornings. He spent money constantly, in the arcades of Piccadilly on treats for himself and gifts for me. I felt excluded – I even felt unhappy with him. I had so little in common with this effete, ostentatious young man. When he went off for weekends to country house parties in Hampshire and Sussex and Kent, I stayed in London. Perhaps I was jealous, peeved because, for the first time since we met, he did not need nor even appear to want me. I began my monograph and regretted the loss of my desk at the Museum.

Summer came late that year and almost overnight. One evening at the beginning of June we went for a walk in Green Park. During the past few weeks, Francis had prattled most of the time, about people and parties, gossip of no consequence. Even as a relaxation, as time-filling, I did not understand how any of it could interest him, this man who had written 'Janus', who had spoken to me so many dark truths. I wonder if I bored him at that time, because I had no taste for frivolity. I think that I was a priggish young man.

But this late, warm evening, he was quite silent. The park was crowded on the edge, and empty towards the centre. The trees were a young, luminous green, throwing their rippling, soft-edged shadows on to the grass. A man passed us smoking a cigarette, and the smoke smelled fresh and nostalgic upon the air.

For some reason, I was uneasy, fearful, I felt sure that Francis would tell me, at any moment now, that he was leaving, that he had grown bored. And however little I was in sympathy with his present mood, that was not what I wanted.

We reached the far edge of the park and turned, like a pair of sentries, began to walk back, this time across the grass. Neither of us had spoken.

Then he said, 'I'm not going to that place tonight.' He had some dinner engagement, I did not know where.

'It's rather late to telephone, isn't it?'

'I shan't telephone.'

I shrugged.

'I've had enough.'

'Of dinner parties?'

He gave me a sideways look and did not answer directly. Instead, he stopped and began to search in his pocket for the small black notebook he always carried, talking as he did so. It was as though, that night, he could not come out with anything, he had to circle round and round it.

'When my grandmother was alive, she had a shelf full of miniature books, the size of a book of postage stamps, bound in leather. There were the works of Shakespeare, and then little volumes of uplifting quotations – On Courage, On Friendship – do you know the sort of thing? Very Victorian. And of course there were quotations from the Bible. I remember it had a marvellous watercolour illustration of the sun setting over still water and all the initial letters decorated. It advised you which passages to read in times of sickness or war or deprivation. She always had them near her, she said they were so *strengthening*.'

We were standing under a horse-chestnut tree and he had the notebook in his hand. I wondered what he was trying to tell me.

'So I have my quotation.'

'Only one?' For I knew how packed his memory was, like a grain store, of poetry and aphorisms. It surprised me that he had troubled to write this one down, and carry it with him.

'It's the one that matters.'

'Then surely you'll have told it to me before.'

'I have never told you.'

I waited. He held the notebook close to him, as though afraid I might try to snatch it away. The sun flamed suddenly brighter, before it began to set, the shape of the trees became more clear, their shadows loomed at us, we were crowded in by trees. We stood there for four or five minutes, long enough for the light to fade as unexpectedly as it had intensified, for the grass to turn grey and the air to cool. I realized that he was no longer looking at his pocket book, he was staring into space, ominously still.

'Francis ...'

He looked without surprise, and his face was strangely tranquil. The edginess, the brittleness of the last weeks dissolved away. He put the book into his breast pocket.

'Aren't you going to read it to me?'

'It wouldn't do you any good.'

A breeze blew across the grass from the darkening lake. The sky was blotted mauve and fondant green.

'We ought to go back.'

He followed me. But at the gates of the park, confronted by the swirl and dazzle of Piccadilly, he stopped again.

'Harvey, will it be all right now?' His voice was full of disquiet.

'What? Nothing's wrong that I know of.'

'But you were going to throw me out. Almost any day. I was waiting for you to tell me to go.'

I was overcome with shame and dismay, not that he was right, but that he had sensed my impatience with his recent mood, that I had failed to conceal what he took for disapproval, though it was only a mild irritation. But that was bad enough, God knew, that was more than he could cope with.

The corners of his mouth were working, he was very pale under the street lamp which flared above our heads.

'I can't go, Harvey. I cannot.'

'There's never been any question of it, don't you know that?'

We went across the road, weaving between cars on their way to the West End, to music and dancing and lights. We went back to Sackville Street.

And four days later, to Kerneham.

The small black notebook is under my hand. He never let me see it. I did not discover the quotation until after his death. But I understand that it was at the forefront of his mind more during the times of frenetic gaiety than those of mental tumult and hopelessness, when I worried over him actively and constantly. How deeply I misunderstood him, for the risk was even greater, when he had appeared to be so well. The lines are from Marcus Aurelius.

'In all you do or say or think, recollect that at any time the power of withdrawal from life is in your hands.'

*

Kerneham.

But the memories of childhood it held for me are lost now, burnt and blackened over by the events of that summer. It had been a place of open spaces and growing things, of subtly coloured fungi discovered among the grasses and copses where hundreds of chirring wrens nested, a place of hot summer days and affection, of oil lamps and, when the rain dropped down like a mantle over the downs, of log fires smelling sweet, oak and ash and pear.

They were memories which hung like an old well-worn, comfortable coat in the back of my mind, I could slip into them and feel contented and careless of the adult world.

I was perhaps a sentimental man. But I know that the old feeling of relief, of arrival home and yet of expectancy, filled me as we turned down the lane leading to the cottage.

I thought it would be a perfect place for Francis. I wanted my past associations with it to filter through to him, so that there would be no break with happiness.

He was writing nothing. I myself was busy, both with the monograph and with the reading and reviews of books on my own subject for the academic journals. I think that I *willed* Francis to be as satisfied with the tenor of our everyday life there as I was, to be building up to some new work, even though, after 'Janus', there might be nothing long for some considerable time, probably years.

At first, he deceived me. He took on the part as I had written it for him. He sat in the garden reading Thoreau, Gilbert White's *Selborne*, the *Oxford Dictionary of Flowering Plants*. He took off his shirt and that sparsely fleshed bone-cage began to tan a little, the surface of his hair was blonded by the sun.

But he would look up at me from time to time and his eyes were enigmatic behind the round spectacles, he half-smiled. He took to reading out to me lists of the names of shrubs, roses, mosses, moths, birds, discussing the beauty of the sound of them, learning their familiar country callings.

It was a game. I did not want to know that. One evening he stood by the honeysuckle which trailed over the side fence, and called to me. His face was contorted with self-mockery, he held an arch, balletic pose, one arm gracefully flung out.

'Don't I look pretty? Aren't you proud of me? Come and pat me on the head, there's a dear.'

I felt despised and uncertain whether he was ridiculing himself or me, or both of us.

'The country life!'

'We can go whenever you want to – if you're bored.'

'Ah, but *you're* not, you're loving every minute of it. You have me in the palm of your hand, my dear – eating out of it.'

'You know perfectly well that's not the way I want things to be.'

'Do I? Well, never mind, I like to watch you pottering about from herb garden to kitchen. Shall we have some cowslip wine? Or keep bees?' He did a somersault and then a cartwheel, at which he was rather good, on the small lawn and then rolled over and lay on his back, arms shielding his face. I did not want to quarrel with him, but I felt unable to defend myself from his taunts in any other way. Except by silence. I sat down in the deckchair. I was reading Wordsworth.

After a moment or two he called softly, cooing like a bird from the thicket.

'Har-vee.'

'What is it?'

'Don't sulk.'

I did not reply.

'Take it on the chin like a man.'

I could not focus my eyes on the page for exasperation and misery. What was I doing here with him when I would be so much happier as I had been in the past by myself? Then I could settle back into this drowsy, contemplative life and come and go as I chose, answerable to or for no one.

Now, he was standing behind my chair. He said, 'Rotten poet,' and before I could stop him, flicked the book out of my hands and tossed it high in the air with the ease of an out-fielder. It went sailing over the hawthorn hedge. I stood up and swung round on him. I have never been so near to violence, though I would only have hit out at him like swatting a fly or smacking an overwrought child. I was nearer, at that point, to telling him to go than ever when things were far more difficult, and distressing with him.

'You really can be a bloody nuisance, Francis.'

'Be he alive or be he dead, I'll grind his bones to make my bread ... only which am I? If you prick me do I not bleed?'

'Stop being so damned pretentious, stop playing games, for God's sake, get on with being yourself, that's quite enough to be going on with.'

'Yes,' he said, as though I had just remarked that the sun was high in the sky. 'Yes, it is.'

'I'm sorry – that was unforgivable.'

'Oh, no. Nothing is ever that.'

'I didn't mean what I said.'

'Then you should have meant it. You should always mean the truth.'

'Francis ...'

'Could we have some tea?'

I was quick enough to snatch at the straw of normality. I wanted to believe that the short argument meant nothing, was simply the inevitable result of friction between two people who live together, closely emotional, and which will from time to time give off sparks. I said, this is nothing, this is normal. I made tea and Francis made toast and ate it thick with butter and honey, the afternoon slipped away. All was well.

But nothing was ever well, one thing led to another, a worse thing. With Francis life was a string of related beads, they grew larger, fatter, darker and then perhaps smaller again, for a short time, a short distance. What you could not do was skip a bead.

But it was early even then, I had still everything to learn.

The next afternoon we walked five or six miles and came out on top of Rake's Barrow. Up here the air was cooler, there was always a mean little breeze snecking at one's hair, no matter how hot and still the day.

There were no trees, no shrubs, no bushes. The track led up in a thin, grey line over the top of the barrow and down, on to the next. There were a few lone flint-stone walls, half-crumbled away after the gales which shrieked over here in winter. All around us the hills were rounded, dark as grapes, spread with coarse heather. The grass was yellow, sapless, the soil showed between like skin between the last hairs on an old man's head. There were a few sheep. And a buzzard, hovering, raking the valley with its close sharp eye.

We were sitting down on a part of the wall. Below us we could see the tree tops, blue-green, the gardens, the glint of a stream, and roofs, slate and thatch and brick, going this way and that, with the brass cock on the church spire shining like a golden angel.

Up here there was never complete silence, the wind always moaned softly. The cry of a sheep came floating to us, sounding, at this height, not inane but sinister. Then, the sun began to go behind a cloud and the great charcoal shadows began to move towards us over barrow after barrow, they were like bats chasing one another, and we were in the very last of the light, and then we too were overtaken, gobbled up by the dusk. I had very often felt the extreme loneliness, the sense of being a tiny thing exposed to all the forces of nature up here. It gave me no more than a shiver when the shadows closed in.

But Francis got up and began to run, he had gone half way down the slope before I realized it and there was panic in his movements, his arms and legs flew out jerkily, his head was thrown back. By the time I caught up with him he had reached the base of the next slope on a narrow track leading towards where the vegetation began again, a cluster of gorse bushes. I put out my hand to touch him but he lurched away, he went on running. His breath came tearing out of his lungs. I was only just keeping up with him, there was a painful stitch in my left side, when, just beside the gorse, he stumbled on a stone and fell headlong, and then he lay there, his face pressed into the dusty bare path, sobbing in an awful, demented way and clawing at the earth with his fingers. I knelt beside him and waited for a long time for him to quieten down. The sun came out again and a pair of dunlin rose and chattered and fell again above the blazing gorse.

He showed no signs of calming. I managed to get him over and sitting upright but at once he bent his head to his knees, rubbing his face over and over again over the rough cloth of his trousers. He was saying something, a jumble of words that made no sense, even when I managed to decipher them. I held on to him and he rocked to and fro with pain and fear. He smelled of sweat that had sprung out of his pores like tears and was now soaking him through. I noticed that his hands were grazed and bleeding a little, the blood was trickling slowly down one arm, mingled with the brick dust.

We must have stayed there for over an hour and he grew not less agitated but more so, he clung on to me and shouted out, screamed, and then began to weep again, and cradling his head between his hands he shook it violently as if to get rid of something clinging like a burr inside.

It was a close evening, there was nothing to slake the dry air and the sunburnt ground and the throbbing of my own head, nothing to cool Francis, to soothe him. I managed, eventually, to get him back to the cottage. By the time we reached it, it was quite dark. We stumbled along the track, I had to lead him as though he had gone blind, and every few yards he would stop and try to get out of my grasp and throw himself down upon the ground again, and then it was as though he were trying to push himself right inside the earth.

I talked to him as one would talk to a frightened horse, I coaxed him with words about the cool house, the drawn curtains, the safety of bed, water to drink, sleep. I was desperately afraid that he might break away from me and run off into the darkness, that he would do himself an injury either on purpose or, more likely in his present, deranged state, quite by accident. I held him and led him as though by a rein and bit.

It was like a nightmare getting him along the lane. He was crying now as if he would never be able to stop, the tears coursing down his face. I wiped them off with my handkerchief, after his own was soaked through.

We reached the house. I got him into a chair, drew the curtains, lit an oil lamp and attended to the cuts on his hands, sponged his face and neck.

He said once, 'Where are we going?'

'Nowhere. You're home with me. You're all right.'

The words had the opposite of a quieting effect. He pushed me violently away from him, the bowl of water went flying all over the chair. He went to the far wall and began to beat his head against it so hard I thought he would break his skull, it took all the strength I had to get him away.

I knew then that he could not be allowed to continue in this way, that, for the moment, I could no longer cope. I poured out a measure of brandy, pushing him into the chair again, and made him drink it slowly, holding the glass to his mouth and tilting his head back, telling him when to swallow. His eyes were red-rimmed and ferine.

The drink eventually began to make him heavy, his head rolled from side to side, out of control. Then I went quickly into the study and telephoned for a doctor I knew, who lived in the town a dozen miles away, explaining about Francis in a low voice, terrified that he would hear. The man said he would come out at once.

When I returned, Francis was crying again, tears of silent misery. I held his hand. He said nothing at all, though the alcohol had not made him sleep, only stilled him a little, he was still tense, still likely at any moment to leap up again and go crazy. I think he had no idea where he was, or who was with him, there was no recognition of anything in his eyes, though I went on talking to him, tried to make him feel safe.

I had told the doctor not to knock but to come straight in as quietly and unobtrusively as he could. When he did so, he took a swift glance at Francis and said, 'We must get him away.'

'No!'

'Look here ...'

'No, I can't have that, I'm sorry. He couldn't take it.'

'You have no idea what you're trying to cope with.'

'Oh yes, I do know.'

'I can inject him and it will last for a few hours, but then ...'

'We'll cross that bridge when I come to it.'

'He needs treatment – more than I can give him.'

'I'm sorry, it's out of the question. I absolutely forbid it. He must stay here. I shall wish I had not called you out.'

He shrugged, went into the kitchen to wash his hands, fitted his syringe together. I knew that he disapproved so much that he would, in all probability, refuse to come out if I ever had to call him again like this, refuse to have anything more to do with the case.

'You realize he may try to kill himself. Or you.'

'I realize that.'

'You're not doing him a good turn, you know.'

I did not answer.

He lifted the sleeve of Francis's shirt and injected him. Francis did not flicker, seemed not to know what was happening.

'Right, we'll get him to bed.'

'I can manage, thanks.'

I had betrayed my first promise to Francis already. I did not want him to have to put up with any more than had been absolutely necessary.

'You're a fool, Lawson. Get him to a hospital, get him committed, for God's sake, it's for his own good.'

I showed him out. I had thought that I could trust him more than this, and now I only wanted him away before Francis realized what had happened.

I got him into the bedroom and undressed him. He was

already half asleep and a dead weight, it was like manoeuvring a corpse. When I let go of his arm it fell and lay inert on the sheet. I washed his face and hands again, brushed back his hair. He was breathing easily, drowned in sleep.

I went back and cleaned up the sitting-room, poured myself a drink. I was delirious with shock and tiredness. But I did not sleep. I could not go on trying. In the end, I simply sat on a chair beside the bed in my dressing-gown, watching Francis.

It was a cold, damp, comfortless dawn which eventually came trailing into the room.

For the next three days, he was in a drugged, twilight state, spending much of the time in bed with the curtains drawn – and missing nothing, for the weather changed, it was gloomy and drizzling, with a strong wind beating the heads off the sunflowers and hollyhocks in the garden. I fed him and he ate everything obediently. I read *The Last Chronicle of Barset* and Pliny's *Natural History* aloud to him. He would scarcely ever look at me. I had no way of knowing whether he remembered anything about that fearful afternoon and night. It was not referred to. The doctor was not mentioned.

Every so often, he would say, 'My head hurts.'

'I can't breathe.'

'The walls are falling in on me.'

And he woke at night constantly, chased down the long tunnels of sleep by howling nightmares and then he held on to me and wept. I thought that I ought to try and get him some sedatives at night, but I would not go back to the doctor who had wanted him committed, nor dared to consult any other, and in any case, with his suspicion of drugs, Francis might not have taken them. I felt entirely powerless to help him be rid of the horrors swirling in his mind. I found him one afternoon sitting and staring at his hands, holding them closely to his face.

'Why am I bleeding?'

'But you're not.' The grazes had been superficial, they were quite healed now.

'Don't be ridiculous, you can see it, look, look – You've got to do something to stop it, I'll bleed to death.'

He scrabbled for his handkerchief and would not be quieted until I had brought a bowl of water and a towel and let him wash himself. What else might he think? How far ought I to pander to his delusions? I had no idea. I could only work by the instinct of the moment.

Then, one day, he got up and dressed very early and said he had work to do. He spent more than four hours sitting at the little oak desk in a dark corner of the living-room, covering several pages of a notebook in a cramped, unsteady hand-writing. Reading it now I see that it is mainly a series of uncon-nected sentences, punctuated here and there by the lists of plant and insect names he had grown so addicted to. But, on two separate sheets of paper, he wrote some fragments of verse in a clearer hand. They bear all the traces of his madness and yet they have a strange, incoherent beauty all of their own, his lyricism and sense of rhythm were as innate to him as breath-ing, and they somehow managed to surface, in these snatches.

There was an old gramophone in the cottage and a cupboard full of my godmother's records, for she had been a woman who determinedly kept up with innovations, she was always the first in the whole county to try out something new – to install gas, buy a crystal set, drive a motor car.

The records revealed rather a limited, sentimental taste: Delibes, Grieg's Piano Concerto, 'Love's Dream after the Ball', Strauss Waltzes, Air on the G String. But besides these there were Victorian drawing-room ballads, generally sung by bass baritones with voices rich as stout, or a fruity contralto, accom-panied by a fluttering, rather sharply tuned piano. Francis would wind up the machine and sit on the floor for hours, putting on one of these songs after another, smiling rather whimsically. I could not bear them and yet they reminded me vividly of my childhood, when I had lain awake in the back bedroom up-stairs and heard the same voices come singing up to me.

'One last touch of your soft, soft hand.'
'Come into the garden, Maud.'
'Dear, as the snowflake settles.'
'Speak, speak, speak to me, Thora.'
To think of them now chills me. How everything altered for

me in that cottage, within the space of a few weeks! Now, when I think of my childhood, there are so many blank spaces, with only odd, affecting recollections, of our London house overlooking the river, or a visit to my governess's parents in Cornwall. Only Christmas remains quite clear and glowing in my mind, for Christmas we always spent with my grandmother Lawson at Putney, a stone's throw away from The Pines, out of which prim-looking house I once saw Swinburne emerge, when I was four or five years old, and was told to remove my cap and bow, as I once bowed, near Westminster Abbey, to the old Queen.

But Putney was over, the house sold long before I met Francis, we never went near to it: nor did Christmas, a season of which, as an adult, I have never been especially fond, ever have any special associations during our time together. I think he may always have been quite well, or else we were abroad, but somehow, Christmas is always left out of it.

The weather improved a little. Francis did not. He was lethargic, sullen, wrapped up in himself, but he burst out occasionally in moments of dread of the torment that was within him, or to come. Then he decided again that he wanted to work, not upon anything of his own, he was not ready for that, but upon some translations. He had me send to London for Rimbaud, Baudelaire and Ovid, and for some Anglo-Saxon poems and riddles of which he was very fond – he had taught himself the language at Oxford.

The books seemed to waken him up, he began to work at fever pitch, getting up early, eating in hurried gulps, piling up dictionaries on his desk. He would make version after version of a single poem, and then keep them all, compiling one final one from the many variations. I tried to get him to relax or walk, or read something light in between times, but he would not, even the gramophone was silent, he drove himself on all day, like a man spurring a horse. It grew hotter again, it was the beginning of August, the bees droned and the leaves of the trees hung heavy and parched, already tipping over from green towards the yellows and browns of autumn. In the evenings, clouds of gnats jazzed about at the bottom of the garden. There were no flowers left in the woods and, apart from the monotonous wood-pigeons and the shrieking of jays, the birds had gone quiet.

So long as Francis behaved so erratically, I myself was on edge, my own work went slowly, I found it hard to concentrate. I was scarcely able to conceal my alarm when, early one afternoon, he said he wanted to go for a walk alone. But I could not prevent him. So I took the garden shears and set about the hawthorn hedge, hoping to dull my anxiety and pass the time in hard physical work.

By six o'clock he had not come back. My hands were calloused and burning, the hedge was over-neat. Then, I heard voices drifting towards me down the lane. I saw Francis, walking rather slowly and holding by the hand, like a devoted mother, Josh, the idiot boy, son of Mead the carter.

Josh was born the year before my godmother died. There was only one more summer to come.

She had to do with the people from the village, but we never did: we were the visitors, the London people. They gave us good-day and no more, although I think they loved my godmother. But it meant nothing that we were close to her. Yet I remember the day of Josh Mead's birth. I was eighteen.

I had been ill for most of that summer with some germ affecting my lungs and I went up on to the barrow as often as possible, for there I could breathe, the raking pain in my chest was eased. And up there, late one afternoon, I met Mrs Mead walking back from Shayle, four miles away on the other side of the slope. Round by the road it was eight miles, but Mead was a carter, and she was nine months pregnant. She came slowly over the path and stopped, resting her arms and basket in front of her, on the enormous belly. She did not look rounded but angular, the child jutted out from below her breast like a shelf. She was ungainly as a cow and when she neared me I saw that she looked old, she might have been fifty, though I suppose she was no more than thirty-one or -two. Her face was reddened and coarsened by the sun and shining with sweat, her hair scraped back and held tightly in a comb. I went to take the basket from her. Her face closed with suspicion.

'You shouldn't be lugging this, you look exhausted.'

'I can manage, thank you.' The thick, West country accent took the edge off what was in fact a sharp rebuff.

'No, you really must let me carry it the rest of the way for you now.'

She shrugged, but would not walk beside me, only a step or two behind. I tried to talk to her. I was indignant that her husband, with several vehicles and horses to take him all over the county, should have let her walk over the barrow alone. But she resented my criticism, she said he'd 'gone working', it was not his job to fetch and carry her about. Nor would she talk about her other three children, and in the end I fell silent. She barely thanked me when we reached their gate. It was a large, ugly cottage at the far end of the village, next to Shenlow's farm. I felt put in my place. I had embarrassed and annoyed her, and it was true that women like Jane Mead did as much work as the men, were just as strong. My chivalrous instincts were town-bred and she scorned them.

The next morning, my godmother came up from the village and told us that Jane Mead had had a son during the night.

'But he won't live and that's as well.'

Josh did live, though my godmother told me that Jane Mead had prayed aloud that he would not. I did not see him until the following year and by that time my godmother was dying, Kerneham was changed, we had no time to worry about the villagers.

But they cared for her. They barely acknowledged us when they came in, knowing that my godmother was dying and making no secret that this was their last visit. And Jane Mead came, bringing Josh. He could not walk and his head was too large, like a tulip unsupported on an etiolated neck. He had a slight hunch on his back and unfocused eyes, he waved his hands about in front of his face as a baby of a few weeks old will do, fascinated by them.

My mother was afraid that my godmother would be distressed. 'They don't *think*,' she said, 'they've no sense in their stupid heads.' For she had never had any time for the village people, would not acknowledge how sharp, or how good some of them were. To her, they were all lower-class bumpkins. But my godmother was not upset by Josh, she took him on to her bed and played with him, I think she felt more affection and sympathy for him than his own family did, for to them he was a stigma, and they were marked out forever as having borne an idiot.

For idiot he was, and as such he was both tolerated and entirely disregarded by the community, he was treated rather like a cow which will not yield, or a backward horse dragging the rest of the team out of true.

Now, he was grown up, he was seventeen, a big-boned, lolling boy, and strong, though still pale. I watched him coming down the lane with Francis. He was smiling and nodding his head. The clothes he wore were cast-offs from his brothers, for he was not considered worthy of anything new and so they were all a size too large or too small for him. The trousers fell in baggy creases like a clown's costume, held up by an old belt.

He had never been to school, never learned to do the simplest of jobs, he could not tie the laces of his own shoes. He often sat in the sun on the churchyard wall, or by Coper's pond, staring ahead of him at the ducks or the gravestones, smiling, smiling, and endlessly fidgeting with his hands.

They reached the gate. Francis said, 'I've brought a friend.'

'Hello, Josh.' I had no idea whether he remembered me from one year to the next. But he was an amiable boy, glad to talk to anyone, go with anyone, though few took any notice of him at all.

He came shambling into the garden. 'Fowers.'

'Do you like flowers?'

He made for the bottom bed, with a curious, sideways gait, and began to grasp at the tallest sunflowers, bending them towards him and putting his face down in them until he sneezed. To reach them he trampled quite unaware all over the soil and the smaller plants.

Francis reached across and began to talk to him and I watched Josh's friendly ugly face as he listened. I saw what had brought them together. They gave attention, total absorption in one another, they were listeners, there was just the same expression of devoted attention on Francis's face when I read to him, if he was ill. But Francis was, though not handsome, co-ordinated, his features looked as if they had been designed to go together.

71

Josh's did not. His mouth was thick and half open, his nose and chin were smudged, as though made of putty thrown on to his face from a distance. His eyes, which had almost no brows or lashes, and very heavy lids, were never quite focused together. I felt sorry for him, he did not repel me, but I could not summon up enough patience, I could not be interested in him or loving towards him as Francis was.

For the next fortnight, he spent a large part of every day with Josh, either at the cottage or out somewhere: they went walking for eight or ten miles at a time. They would sit on the lawn for hours, while Francis tried to teach him the difference between various flowers, or showed him how to make a circle, a square and a triangle with pebbles. What Josh liked best, he said, was to find a stream and sit with his shoes off watching the water slide over his feet, or else taking a handful of pebbles and dropping them in one by one, making bigger and smaller splashes. Josh liked noise, making a noise. I remembered Francis at the piano.

They strung up a row of mugs on a line across the kitchen, and Josh would stand hitting them with a wooden spoon, enchanted by the vibrant, bell-like sounds, and when he was shown how to run the spoon quickly along the row, like a xylophone, he was beside himself, he laughed and made odd grunts and snorts of pleasure and stayed there for the rest of the day, until I thought I would be driven mad by the sound.

Josh stayed to meals and ate with his hands and threw the food about, ground it into a mess on the tablecloth, but it was Francis was patiently cleared up after him, and Francis who showed him how to hold a spoon and then a fork, and eat with them neatly. It was his triumph. Josh was delighted with himself, he took the spoon and fork home, wrapped in brown paper, and brought them back each time.

When he was not with us, Francis scarcely mentioned Josh. He seemed better in himself, he had begun to read again, and he talked normally, the nightmares began to lessen.

Then, one morning, he came back from the village with tears streaming down his face, beating his fists upon his thighs in anger. Jane Mead had refused to let Josh come out with him.

'Why, Harvey, why? What am I supposed to have done? I'm

the only person who pays any attention to him or takes any
trouble, I'm the only person he cares about.'

I said gently, 'Perhaps that's why they resent you.'

'How can they?'

'He is theirs, however little they seem to regard him. Perhaps
you've made them feel inadequate.'

'God damn it, they *are* inadequate.'

'I know – but they are his family too.'

'Oh, you as well, you believe in all that, do you? In flesh and
blood being thicker than water. I never thought I'd hear it all
coming from you.'

'Francis, you know what I mean and what I don't mean. You
must try and see that to them, however crazy Josh is, he is
their boy and his place is with them and you've been trying to
take him away – to take his affection away.'

'But they don't do a thing for him. They just leave him to
sit and moon at the pond, they shovel food into him because it's
too much trouble to teach him to hold a spoon.'

'I know.'

'What is he going to think? When they say he can't come
with me, can't come here and be with us? How is he going to
feel? Because I know, I know how I should feel.'

But Josh did not and Francis could never take it in. He
thought that Josh was like himself, but Josh was quite different.
He had enjoyed the walks and the meals and the attention. Now
they were withdrawn. But it was all the same with him. He
lived from moment to moment, he could not relate past to
present, nor see ahead into the future. He simply forgot about
the days with Francis, I think. He was quite happy to go back
to his roaming around their garden and yard, or sitting smiling
into the pond. He would smile at us, too, if we went by, he
smiled at anyone.

Francis was bitterly hurt. I do not think he ever accepted
that Josh was quite careless of him : he blamed the Meads, who
had, he said, poisoned the boy's mind, intimidated him, turned
Josh against him.

And so began that paranoia, which was never really to leave
him, only to lie dormant occasionally, for the rest of his
life.

Nothing had been said about our leaving Kerneham. August was glazed and dry. Towards the end of the month, a letter came for Francis from Fowlers. The first proofs of 'Janus' were ready. The managing editor, Harold Simmons, wanted to come down and see him, so that he could go over the poems and discuss the next volume of shorter pieces.

I thought that Francis was quite up to it. He seemed to have put Josh out of his mind. He was sunbathing most of the days, and reading Plato and Dickens. He had done about thirty very beautiful translations of the French, Latin and Anglo-Saxon poems and he wanted to show them to Fowlers, with the idea of publishing them at first in a limited, expensively bound edition. His reputation, once 'Janus' was out, would be consolidated, he was sure of that, he was no longer the bright, promising young man, one of the good war poets, he had gone on from there, matured and written something really fine.

The idea of the handsomely presented translations appealed to him. He had always loved beautiful books, though rather as art objects that had nothing much to do with literature. He was knowledgeable on the subject of engravers and type-faces, hand-made paper. He wrote to Simmons, making a date for the following week.

I was relieved. At last things seemed to be on a more even keel. I was happy for him. And happy with him. He made me laugh a great deal, he said wise things, he was thoughtful, gentle, kind and loving to me. How could I fail to respond?

*

Friday

Christ came into this world to save sinners and they have prevented me, I would have given all the love and forgiveness that I have in me to the boy for whose release I was born and they have filled my mouth with spawn and ashes to spit upon one who needs me.

Burn, for the fire is a very pure and constant light, the fire devours all uncleanness, the fire is my true friend.

I have wasted years of my life.

A hunchback was a lucky man, if you touched a hunchback he brought you good fortune and health and freedom from bad dreams. Therefore, come in file and each shall touch the hunch-back and peace be to him.

But I am for hell.

Sunday

I wish they would stop ringing those bloody bells.

But one day I shall write a great poem, fire and water and the lord and giver of life and all manner of growing, creeping things and the boy with the crooked back.

Green that is green but that is blue, would you say the clear water is blue?

Tuesday

H. will not believe me about the bells that won't stop ringing, and they are NOT IN MY HEAD. He thinks they are only in my head but they are bells in the air, all the churches from the barrow to Wendon Point are pealing their bells for weddings and rejoicings or tolling for all the drowned dead of the world.

A man that is drowned has the sweetest dreams.

Friday

A letter from Simmons, who will come here. The proofs of 'Janus' are ready. I like Simmons, he's an honest tradesman. That is all I have to say. That is a mighty poem, but I cannot bear to look at the words of it on the page and now they want more, they want to take their hooks and push them up my nostrils and pull down my brain, they would poke and pry inside me and get their greasy fingers on to my work. They will come here and talk and whisper like the grass in corners and take away all my papers and laugh about them, passing them around in their circles, their magic ring. Pass the parcel, and when the music stops, who shall win?

Well, they will not have them, they shall not see.

But Harvey may see. Oh, he comes into the room and goes out of the room and he is a charmed man, I will only lie with him and the rest will be rotted and burned. Then we shall be free and there will be nothing but sweet air between us, then we shall live forever and ever.

Saturday

My neck burns and aches, my eyes sting as though I have a fever. H. takes my temperature and makes cool drinks, and I will one day look after him in return, when he is an old, old man, strength always to ...

Simmons comes on Thursday.

I wish we had a cat or a dog, I would like to hold a furred thing close up to my face. I walk into the fields and go up to the young cows and put my face on their warm coarse necks. But they rear away, they are afraid of me. Why are they afraid? Because I tried to kill my brother.

There are foxes beyond the barrow with eyes like candles, they live secret, sidling, quick-fire lives. H. says we shall go into the woods at Grotham one night to look at the badgers. He went when he was a boy, with Rex, the gamekeeper's son from Bodeley. He is a countryman, he should never live in towns.

Well then, we shall stay here forever, I shall have no other life. It will be best for me. Only I wish for water, for a boat to row upon a lake.

I shall write some short pieces about the foxes of Kerneham and the buzzards and sparrow-hawks and kestrels over the barrow. I love the falcon birds, the hunters. I love their evil, their steeliness, the way they rise to a great height all alone and the beauty of their fall, slow or quick, the arrow grace of their swoop down upon prey.

There are three trees loaded down with crab apples. This morning I took off my shirt and climbed up and picked them, in a basket, we had eleven pounds, and so H. goes down to the village and buys sugar, and boils away and now it is all dripping and straining through a muslin bag and the kitchen smells warm and sweet and cidery, we shall have hundreds of jars of jelly all glowing and clear as berries. I have this afternoon got down and washed and dried all the jars. These things are very good, coming upon us, and soon it will be September, that Samuel Palmer month.

Là, tout n'est qu'ordre et beauté,
Luxe, calme et volupté.

I have a devil's claw upon my forehead.

*

On the day before Harold Simmons was due, Francis spent two or three hours writing out labels for the crab apple jelly. He lettered them in that graceful, idiosyncratic hand, in black, and made a symbol like a seal mark underneath.

After lunch he slept in the garden while I wrote letters. It was a golden, late summer day, with a touch of wood-smoke in the air. Towards evening the light faded to a pellucid blue and the moon and stars were out before it had gone. A bullfinch had been singing from far away, like notes played upon a wooden flute.

Francis opened his eyes but stayed, quite relaxed for a while, watching the sky.

I said, 'Mind you don't get a chill. It suddenly drops down cold on these sort of evenings.'

He smiled, and I heard myself fussing over him. 'You look all right,' I acknowledged, 'I don't know why I worry.'

'Never mind.'

I stretched. The letter pad slithered off my knee.

'We won't ever leave here, will we?'

'Not if you don't want to. But you might change your mind in the winter. It snows a lot, it gets cut off here usually, for weeks at a time. Not so much fun then.'

'We shall see. Who are you writing to?'

'My father.'

'Why?'

'He's an old man. He likes to know I'm around.'

'Do you love him?'

'Yes.'

'Why?'

I shook my head.

'Just because he's your father and you're his little boy?'

'No. I love him for what he is. I love him more now than I did when I was a child. He's a good man, though he can be a tiresome one. And he hasn't been well – really, it's time I went to see him.'

Francis lay absolutely still.

77

'Perhaps I should take you.'

'Oh no.'

'Well – I ought to go for a day or two sometime soon. Next month. Should you mind?'

'It's nothing to do with me.'

'I mean should you mind staying here alone?'

'I got along perfectly well without you once upon a time, you know.'

'Good. So it would be all right.'

'No man is indispensable.'

'I never supposed that I was.'

Francis leaped to his feet and screamed, roared at me. 'Will you bloody well stop agreeing with me all the time, stop behaving like a little puppy dog.'

There was never any point in my saying anything in reply to this kind of outburst. I was hurt and angry and weary of it. But I also suspected that he might be right, though I could not really help how I behaved towards him. I wanted him to stay calm, I wanted peace, a quiet life. It seemed best to humour him.

I said, 'It's getting colder. I'm going in.'

He came over and leaned against me, his shirt was already faintly damp to my touch.

'Come on.'

'I'm very tired. I'm so tired I can't breathe.'

'Go to bed now, then – I'll bring you in something to eat if you like.'

'Why should you?'

'Why shouldn't I?'

But in fact he stayed up, he built a fire of ash logs in the old grate and tended it like a mother hen, with the poker and bellows. We had left the window open and moths came in to bat furrily against the lamp. It was an easy, placid, unremarkable evening. Francis sang to himself softly as he got ready for bed.

I woke, not because there was a sound in the room but because there was not. Francis was not there. He was nowhere in the cottage. It was just after two o'clock.

The night outside seemed to be still and yet full of rustling, furtive creatures hidden here and there in the undergrowth and grass banks, or above me in the sycamore and elm trees. I saw the red glimmering eyes of a stoat, as its thin form snaked across the road almost under my feet. Bats were swooping crazily in the air unseen, only making a sudden breath on my face as their wings brushed close by me.

I felt spied upon as I walked down the lane, watched by small eyes everywhere. Movements were frozen as I passed. I thought of the teeming insect and amphibious life in the ditches, of all the activity one never saw, never knew about. It was cool and there was a faint mistiness in the air, the outline of the full moon was fuzzed at the edges.

I had no idea which way to go first. I stopped and tried to strain an ear for some sound of him, to sense which way he had gone. Nothing. I walked down through the village. The houses were drained of colour, grey and chalk-white with blank, black windows. The barns were full of silver hay. There was no sound, no sign of Francis. The dog barked from Shenlow's farm, a high, yelping, warning note, and from somewhere in the woods a fox answered.

I walked back, flashing my torch here and there, so that a patch of hawthorn hedge would be illumined, and every detail of twig and the underside of leaf showed up, the bells of the convolvulus shone white as paper.

Up on the barrow I sensed that uneasiness which is breathed in with the air. This countryside had been part of my growing, I had inhaled its ghosts along with the shapes and sounds. There were innumerable local stories about the spirits of the barrow : shepherds who had died in the blizzards of winter and were found again the following spring, their bones picked clean : travellers lost, led by Jack o'Lanterns into hidden peat bogs, witches hounded out of their mud and stone shelters after the sudden, unaccountable death of a child, and taken down the hill to be branded and ducked and burned. None of the people of Kerneham would have come up here alone at night, or perhaps even in groups, men or women. But Francis would come. I went for a long way, flashing my torch every now and then. A fox slipped by me, the light catching on its brush. Once or twice

I called out but my voice echoed and came back to me from miles away, I was unnerved by it. Besides, he would be hiding somewhere, he would not have answered.

The heather was tangled when I got off the track, several times I tripped and half fell. It was even mistier up here, the air was soft and clammy against my face. I was afraid of going too far and losing my way, and when the moon finally sank behind clouds, I turned round again.

I went back to the cottage and made myself a pot of coffee and drank it with some rum, waited. The log fire had slipped and crumbled low in the grate, and when I touched it with the poker, the whole collapsed into a grey-white dust, like a skeleton moved from its coffin after hundreds of years. I built up a small fire again and sat watching it spark and falter, then begin to glow crimson. I could not do anything, could not think or read, I only waited, alert, tense as one of the animals I had disturbed outside in the night.

By five in the morning, Francis had still not returned. I might have begun to alert people, make up a party of searchers, but that would have been fatal, if a stranger were to come upon him when he was in distress of some kind, I could not guess at the consequences. What baffled me was the fact that he had been so well and tranquil the previous evening, as though nothing could ever touch him again.

Then I thought of the churchyard. I had not been so far up the slope in that direction. But it was the kind of place where he might chose to spend a distraught night in one of his morbid fits. I was so certain that I was right, it was like a revelation, I ran headlong down the lanes, my feet pounding, so that Shenlow's dog began to bark again furiously this time, certain of danger.

He was not in the churchyard. Each rounded gravestone showed mould and moss green under my torch. In places the grass had grown long, sorrel and dock sprouted from the crevices and the stones were broken like old teeth. I stumbled, out of breath, more desperate and full of panic than I had been all night. He was nowhere, nowhere.

I went into the church itself and found him at once, huddled up like a foetus, cold and stiff with exhaustion and terror. He began to tell me that he was better here, he was safe, he ought to be locked away, why had I left him to do it himself?

But he came quietly enough back to the cottage with me, the first light was seeping over the barrow, mushroom-grey, the hedges were soaked with bead curtains of damp, the misty air tasted metallic. Francis was dressed only in cotton trousers and an open shirt, his flesh was cold as marble.

He had a bath and sat by the fire, which was blazing high, drinking tea, quite silent. I wanted to ask what had been wrong, what was burning inside his head. He was gaunt and tall and insubstantial as a spectre, sitting in the high-backed chair, his hands stretched out towards the fire. The steam rose up into his face from the cup, misting his spectacles, so that he had no eyes, no sight, nor could I look into his, he was quite shuttered, hidden, inaccessible to me.

I sat down beside him. 'Francis, shall I telegraph to Simmons and put him off?'

He removed the glasses so that he peered at me like a mole, he looked defenceless. 'No, it's all right. I'm all right now.'

'Are you sure? He can just as well come another day.'

'No, I want to see him.'

'All right.'

Simmons was due by the eleven thirty train. Mead would fetch him from the station at Shayle. At a quarter past, Francis was still sitting, half asleep, by the fire, not yet dressed. Outside, the sun had emerged, in rays thin as pencils spearing down through the mist. I came from the kitchen to rouse him. 'Yes,' he said, 'you must tell me what to do, you must help me. No one helps me now.'

But when he went into the bedroom he locked the door behind him, I heard the basin taps being turned on.

At five to twelve, Harold Simmons arrived. I had only met him once before and liked him greatly. He was not old, perhaps forty, but entirely bald, with a very high, domed forehead and a wide, rosy-red mouth. He looked out of place in Kerneham, with his formal well-cut suit and watch chain, his stiff collar.

Francis was still in the bedroom. It was hot now, the last of the fog had rolled back and dissolved behind the barrow and the sun was high in the sky. I brought a chair on to the terrace, gave him a drink and went to warn Francis. He did not reply but I could hear movements within the room.

Half an hour passed. We had each drunk two large glasses of sherry. I had explained a little about how Francis had been, but rapidly, in low tones, afraid of betraying him, afraid that he would come out and hear me.

Simmons said, 'This is a fine poem. It's a *great* poem.' He touched the briefcase which held the proofs of 'Janus'. 'The early things were marvellous – fresh, lyrical, intelligent, but they were only preludes, one would not really have predicted such a thing as this, from what went before. There's a power, a depth of emotion and thought, yet all highly ordered and all quite beautifully observed. It's enigmatic, it's difficult beyond words, in places – it will take years for it to be understood fully – perhaps it never will be. But there's no doubt in my mind that it's a poem of genius. I had thought him talented, highly talented, but this puts him on an altogether different plane.'

'He's been writing some other things since we came here.' But I did not go on. It was for Francis to talk to him about his work as he thought best, not for me.

At that moment I heard him unlock the bedroom door. I was relieved, I had been worried, after the previous night, what he might be doing, even whether he would come out at all. But all the same I was quite unprepared for him.

The bedroom wardrobes and cupboards contained, among other things, some old clothes of my godmother's husband, Brent, which she either could not bear or did not know how to dispose of. They were mostly in cardboard boxes, neatly folded and layered with tissue paper, preserved in moth balls. Francis had found them.

Or, to be exact, he found a morning suit, a magnificent, full-dress morning suit, made by a St James's tailor, for Brent had been a rich and rather vain man. The suit fitted Francis reasonably well, though the sleeves of the pale grey jacket were a little short. He had on the cravat, held with a diamond pin, gold cuff links, silk socks. He looked more elegant, more handsome, than I had ever seen him, even during the sociable weeks in London. He also looked ludicrous, pathetic, crazy, I wanted to weep for him. Harold Simmons had taken the situation in at once, he stood up without hesitation and held out his hand. Francis took it, bowed very low, and kissed it.

He said, 'My dear man, I'm most awfully sorry, the valet kept me waiting, he got everything wrong, and then I had an audience with the Archbishop. I hope they've been looking after you. Do sit down.'

Simmons sat. Francis remained standing, his face set in a polite, Royal half-smile. There was complete silence. My head span. I felt a lurch of sickness in my stomach. A blackbird perched on the gatepost and began to sing a full, rich, elaborate melody.

Nothing, of course, could be done that day about 'Janus', the poem was not even mentioned. Francis insisted upon taking Simmons on a perambulation about the garden, measuring the way up and down with great solemnity, holding his arm and inclining politely towards him when he spoke. I wondered fleetingly whether he might not, in fact, be quite sane and knew perfectly well what he was doing, whether this was one of his elaborate games, aware as I was of his fascination with mask and face, appearance and disguise. It was impossible to tell.

He came to me in the kitchen. 'We are ready for luncheon.'

He met my eye quite readily and there was complete honesty in his own, no suggestion of humour or mockery. I nodded.

But after lunch, he vanished again into the bedroom, excusing himself with a great show of courtesy. I looked at Simmons.

'He has never been like this before. This is new.'

'He is very ill. I think.'

'Yes, he ...'

But I was suddenly too weary to explain the events of the night before. Throughout the meal, Francis had kept up a stream of excited, maniacal conversation, darting from subject to subject, half-finishing sentences, often not making any sense at all, rarely waiting for our replies.

'What are you going to do?'

'What can I do?' I asked defensively. 'He is happiest here with me.'

'Is that the best thing for him?'

'I think so. It isn't an easy judgement to make.'

'I think you're right, Harvey. If you can stand it.'

I wondered, momentarily, if I could.

'What about these new poems?'

Francis came out again, he shouted at us, 'What poems? There are no poems, what are you two whispering about me for, why are you standing there with your heads together? I know, I can't be deceived, but you're too stupid to see it. Well, why don't you go off together, why don't you go back to London, it's what you want, look at you.'

He had taken the morning suit off and was wearing only his blue swimming shorts.

'There aren't any bloody poems, do you hear?'

Simmons nodded.

'I know about the letters you've been writing to one another, I know, I've read them, I've got friends here, they meet me at night, they bring me letters. I don't have to bribe them, they do it for me. Anything. They show me what you write about me and they tell me what you say. There are badgers in the wood but he won't take you to see them, you needn't bother to ask, it's me he wants to take. He wants me.'

'That's all right, Francis.'

'Don't talk to me like that, don't talk to me as if I were a little child. It's what *he* does.'

He walked out of the room into the garden, where he lay down on his stomach in the full sun, arms outstretched.

'He'll make himself ill. Oughtn't he to have a shirt on?'

'Yes, but there's nothing I can do when he's like this.'

'Has it been as bad as this for long?'

'It goes in bouts. I never know what to expect. He was all right yesterday evening – he was really quite well.'

'Will you show me the poems, Harvey?'

I hesitated. I knew where they were, I could even see them, in a blue folder on top of the desk.

I shook my head. 'He has to be able to trust me.'

'Quite. Well – can you try and persuade him to send them to me, when he's well again?'

'Of course I will try. What about "Janus"?'

'We'll leave it a week or two. If you think you can cope with the proofs, telephone me, otherwise they must go off as they are. I'll make sure there are no misprints or literals of course. But he really ought to have the chance to alter anything if he wants to.'

'I'm sorry – you've had a wasted day.'

'Not wasted. Upsetting.'

'Yes. It is.'

We went out into the garden again.

'I'm going, Francis.'

There was no reply. I bent down. Francis was sound asleep. I got a shirt from the house and laid it over his back which was already tinged pink.

I stood up. 'Harold, you knew him long before I did. Has he been like this before?'

'Not so far as I know. I've seen him very excited, and also very low and depressed. But that's fairly normal and in any case, I put it all down to the after-effects of the war. He was at the Somme.'

'He says that has nothing to do with it, that it didn't worry him. That he was happy then. I think he means it.'

'He does. Consciously. There were all sorts of good reasons why he was happy in the army. But you've read the war poems. Form your own conclusions.'

I said despairingly, 'I wonder if it can get any better. Or only worse. I dare not imagine the future.'

'No.'

I walked down to the village with him in the still, shimmering afternoon. The trees were tobacco-coloured at the edges, the rowan already bright with berries.

I said, 'I'll do what I can about the poems.'

Simmons frowned with concern. 'Don't try to do too much, Harvey, don't push yourself too far. No one would expect it of you.'

'Francis does.'

I saw him off with Mead, the horse's hooves kicking up the reddish-brown dust down the lane. Then, the air settled back, everything was quiet again, and I felt unable to move from my place in the sun. Shenlow's dog lay long as a shadow, nose to the ground, and a white cat, swollen with kittens, was slumped heavily near by, basking in the heat.

And I could not bear it any longer, could not bear the loneliness of the place and the strain of living with Francis, could
not bear any more of these glaring days. Harold Simmons had
reminded me too much of normality, of easy conversation and
common sense. For the first time I thought of my old life with
real regret: the exchanges of scholarly minutiae in a museum
doorway, the desk of my study in Sackville Street, with the
lamp shining down on an Egyptian scroll, the quiet, friendly
luncheons with a few friends, the galleries, the occasional
country weekends. On one of which I had met Francis. Why?
Why no one before, and why not someone who was less
demanding, less chafing on the nerves?

Francis.

The mud patches were dried and cracked in the lane, the
colour of dung. The birds were all silent, hidden in the depths
and coolness of the wood.

I went slowly back. Francis was still asleep on the lawn. It
had been a dead-end of a day, nothing accomplished.

In the middle of that night, he went outside again. When I
found him he had already got the bonfire well alight kindling
it with dry bits of twig and piles of leaves. He was bent down
low and his face, illuminated by the orange flames, was quite
mad, he was entirely preoccupied. By the time I got to him he
had already burned all the translations and a number of his own
recent poems, together with notes for both, some of his notebooks and diaries, letters, the working notes for 'Janus'. Now,
he was ripping pages from a book about grasses, and feeding
them jubilantly, one by one, into the flames. He was wearing
only his pyjamas, his feet were bare and his hair and face
stained with smoke and sweat, his eyes glistened.

It was a frightening, demonic scene, the smell made me
think suddenly of bodies burned at the stake and the people
dancing round, of black magic.

When I tried to rescue what I could of the papers, and put
out the fire, Francis fought me off viciously, tearing at me with
his nails and trying to bite me, in a frenzy. I had to let him go.
He was not satisfied until he had burned everything then, he

crouched like a prehistoric hunter, staring at the dying fire, watching it slip down into itself.

When it was dark again, he let me lead him back indoors. He smelled acrid and at the same time damp from the night air, his hair was quite wet.

The next morning he slept late and when he woke, he was very hungry and seemed to have no recollection whatsoever of the previous night. I had gone down before he had wakened and stared down into the ashes, stirring them with a stick. Only a few blackened flakes of paper floated up slowly and sank again, there was nothing that could be salvaged.

*

Beyond the window I can only see the snail-grey sky, and teeming rain, the glass is riven by it. All the waders have flown inland, seagulls hang about the house. It might be winter, though it is still July. There is a wind tearing across from the estuary, beating at the doors.

'You really ought to try and let me have something. There's such a widespread *interest*.'

For Harold Simmons is here, and he has not aged as I have, though he is nearly eighty-four. He has not bent over and sunken into himself, he is steady on his feet, clear-eyed, he has a portliness which is becoming, his cheeks are a little red.

'You are old Father William.' But I am the one who is old.

'I understand how you feel, of course I do. But you are the *only person left who knows*.'

I hold my hands out, my old cracked hands towards the fire. I am very tired. There does not seem to be any time at all now between being tired and being tired.

'You were there. You remember.'

'I was not with him all the time. I scarcely saw him, you know, and when I did – well, he didn't say much to me. I was never close to him. I could never really say, you see, that I *knew* him. I could never say that.'

'I don't want them here, turning over old stones and peering underneath.'

'They will only do what you want.'

'I do not want them to come.'

'I meant that they will suit your convenience, let you say what you want to say, let you rest when you're tired They won't bother you.'

'It is all a bother ... it is ...'

There are times when it is too much even to finish a sentence. I am slipping into silence.

'It could take as long as you liked, they would do a little each day, just according to how you felt.'

Oh, Simmons, you are still a man with both feet in life, you are still looking forward. Argument, persuasion, *business*, are the matter of existence to you, you care, to you Francis is still here.

Yet to me, too, Francis is always here.

'You should move to a warmer place, Harvey, it's bleak here in the winter. You're so far away from everyone.'

Ah, yes.

But the fire is a comfort. Mrs Mumford makes a good fire.

A mistle-thrush hops across the soaking lawn, dun-coloured as the marshes under the rain. A bad-tempered bird.

'Well – I don't want to press you. If you feel you're not up to it, that's that. I don't want to persuade you to do anything against your will.'

From somewhere, then, I summon up a flicker of energy, sufficient to feel the responsibility of it, to be dutiful.

'But do they *care* about Francis? Do they understand him at all? Do they truly care?'

Simmons nods, hands crossed over his belly.

You never understood. You are a good enough man, but you did not *know*.

It is only six o'clock and already as dark as thunder, the mist has fallen lower. On such a day as this, Francis would have gone out, huddled into an oilskin, like a golden plover in the middle of the fen, and stalked for miles between land and sea.

'I suppose there would be microphones.'

'Just one tape recorder.'

'I don't think much of the sound of my own voice.'

No, for I quaver now, and sometimes my teeth become dislodged, I have to ferret around with my tongue. I am appalled at myself.

He spreads his hands out and inspects them, lays them in his lap. He has always been vain about his hands. 'No one wishes to make you do it. You must use your own judgement.'

But I no longer know what my judgement is, whether I am really caring about Francis or about myself, because I am old and do not want to be disturbed. All around me they are slapping my hands and pinching my cheeks, they are telling me to, Wake up, Come along, Wake up, but what I want to do is to slip down again and sleep, sleep.

In a few moments, I will ask him to put on the lamps, for he is suppler than I am, proud of his faculties, he will spring up and trot happily about the room.

'Let them come, let them come.'

His eyes are closed. He leans back in his chair, a man who has won a battle.

*

'Mr Lawson, did he always show his poems to you the moment they were finished?'

'Did he make very many versions of a particular poem?'

'How many?'

'How long did it take him to write "Janus"?'

'What, in your opinion, is "Janus" about? Briefly.'

'Did he write when he was mad?'

'In exactly what ways was he mad? Manic? Suicidal? Paranoiac? Did he have hallucinations? Was he excessively religious?'

'How often was he violent? *How* violent was he?'

'Why did you go to live in Germany during the 1930s?'

'How exactly did he die?'

'I believe that rather a lot of poems were lost. Had he shown you these poems? Were they major works? Were there no versions left of them at all? Did you not feel it was your duty to try and salvage them?'

'Were you closer to him than anyone else in his life?'

'Why did he have so little to do with his family?'

'You travelled together a good deal. Did he enjoy travelling? Had he some grudge against his own country? How could he afford to travel so much?'

'What do you think of his fellow war poets?
of his contemporaries after the war?
of poetry today?'
'Was he the greatest poet of this century?'
'Was he a genius?'
'Would he have been greater if he had been sane?'
'Why did he not go into a hospital during the last years of his life?'
'Did you not try and persuade him to do so?'
'How *exactly* did he die?'
'He went to America for a short time. You stayed in England. Why was that? What effect did America have on him?'
'What *kind* of man was he?'

Francis would have screamed, he would have attacked them. But I am silent. My brain spins. I feel I shall fall or faint or explode within me, I cannot bear it. I am incoherent. I mumble into their steel machine and I avert my face from their eager, leering faces, from their lips that form the terrible questions and now I know how it was with Francis, what he felt when there was a pressure inside his head, when he could hear voices, could not bear the light, wanted to get away, away. I know why he thought that they were whispering about him in corners, I know that they do not understand.

Go away from here. Leave us. Leave us alone.

But I do not say it. I answer them. I make up something, there is a reply to every question, though it is lies, all of it.

'What about his notebooks and diaries? Are you editing them? Did he give instructions to you about them? Will you leave them to a university? What will happen to his papers?'

'There are no papers.'

I lie in bed tightly bound in by sheets, my arms by my sides, as I will lie in my coffin and all is cool and dark and silent.

I shall sleep.

I do not sleep.

For the first time in many years I weep, not for Francis but for myself, for the loss of him.

•

'Which poets did he admire?'

'Did he know many poets?'

'What kind of novels did he read?'

'Was he interested in English philosophers as well as German?'

'How much did he know about natural history? Why does it play such a large part in his work? Do you think he is the last of the Romantic poets?'

'Did he like music?'

'Was he a generous man?'

'Was he an abstemious man?'

'Had he many other friends?'

'Did you have friends in Germany?'

'Did his family resent you?'

'What sort of things did you talk about together?'

'You were an Egyptologist of some repute when you met him. Did you sacrifice much of your own work during your years with him? Do you resent this? Was he interested in your work at all?'

'Did he like dogs?'

'Did he like cats?'

'Do you miss him?'

There is no one who can help me. Mrs Mumford will come to make tea and sandwiches, they will eat my food in short, snapping bites and taste none of it, their feet will mark the carpets of my house forever, the stains are like blood and will never wash away. The room is filled with them, they seem to be growing in size, their feet and legs are elephantine under my table and I am shrinking. I cannot bear them.

They are gone.

A tern flies slowly over the house and away towards the estuary, where the sky shines like a silver coin. I eat a plate of raspberries, dry and hairy, I take one between my fingers and dip it into the sugar and push it into my mouth. I make the bowlful last for a long time. Raspberries taste of summer. Francis said that he would keep a garden full of nothing but raspberries, if he could be bothered to take the trouble over them. But never strawberries. 'Like fat red lips with cotton wool in the middle.'

I have read 'Janus' over again and it is like discovering a new world, I understand it, now that I am an old man.

*

Harvey,

Do not apologize, do not reproach yourself, do not try and justify yourself. You should have gone to see your father, of course, you wanted to go. You should have gone. When have I ever tried to prevent you living your life? Oh God, I read that over, and I know what I am like, how I have made you suffer. I know.

Thank you for writing so often. And I am really perfectly well, they ought to let me home. Having one's appendix out is simply nothing, when you consider what a puny, starveling useless part of one it is and how much appalling pain and misery it can cause, while it's there. It is like a demon, one is far better rid of it, and what exorcism could be cleaner than that of the knife?

You know how much I dream, what bad dreams I sometimes have? But under the anaesthetic I did not dream at all and now I do not dream here at night. And the trees are beautiful to look at beyond my window and I am on my feet for a little now and then and otherwise reading.

There is an old man come into the next bed called Horatio, after Nelson and he is 92 and has had, I think, a part of his gut removed. He is marvellous. He lies and recites to me. 'Are you interested in poetry at all?' he said and when I told him yes, he said, 'Ah, that's a good sign, an excellent sign, the young don't know what poetry is nowadays. I shall give you some poetry.' And he puts his head back and looks at the ceiling and recites – the Ancient Mariner, and Sir Patrick Spens and the burial of Sir John Moore, and the Wife of Usher's Well. Oh, it is marvellous, I love him, and he is so delighted to have an audience. The nurses come and hush him when he gets to the roaring bits in the battle poems. He is very fond of battle poems.

Then he talks to me about his garden. Until a few years ago

he worked for some grandee, an Archduke or the White Queen or whatever, and he tells me about the other gardeners and the boys under him, and how he used to talk to the plants to make them happy and grow, and spat on the weeds and put curses on them, and how flowers have personalities, and temperaments, like children. But he does not like birds, they pick at the seeds and ruin everything, and he thinks that birds look ridiculous. I shall have to teach him a thing or two.

I feel well, a little weak in the knees but not in the head, no, no, I have a head of the best bone material, a poor thing, sir, but mine own – for the present.

How can I tell you how good you have been to me?

Simmons sends me the cover for 'Janus' which is black and white and plain and sounds like a newspaper but is not. I am pleased with it. One wants the riches to be on the inside.

I am very much afraid of what they will say about it. There is no good in believing *they* don't matter and can't hurt me because they do and can and it can live or die, sink or swim, they have such power in their little fingers.

I most fear that they will think it wilfully obscure, that they will dislike the colloquialisms ('not *poetry*') and misunderstand the metaphors and miss the allusions, that they will not *work* at it. Of course the common man will not take to it but it is not for the common man, though perhaps other things of mine may be more popular. I do not despise them. But I must say what is in me and what seems to be the truth and that is not common. Imagination, memory, the musical gift, that is all. And the eye which links not A to B but A to P or Z, which is rarer.

Harvey, where shall we go? We must go away. 'Janus' is out in January and I must get away before that. I shall be leaving hospital in a week more and ready to travel, I suppose, in another week or so after that. Shall you be done with the family? Shall we go to London first and hear some opera? Then to Venice. But perhaps not Venice till mid-October or a bit later?

But I will go anywhere at all with you and you shall choose, it is your turn, I shall do what you want. I am an ungenerous man.

Only that I must go sometime to Venice.

*

Wednesday

'Thou hast commanded that an ill-regulated mind should be its own punishment.'

So it is a *punishment*? I should like to know for what. Ah, for being born, for the original sin. Or else 'Thou' is not 'Thou, God' but 'Thou, Devil' for the Devil has his ten commandments.

H. is back. I have missed the sound of him about the flat, the bump of his hip as he shuts the kitchen drawer, the way he says 'Ah-ha' as he turns a page, though it is nothing, not a comment or a sigh.

This is still *his* flat, not mine, I am only camped here, as I was in Suffolk and Dorset and I will be in Venice I suppose, for of course he has a friend or someone who will lend us a place to stay. H. has a million friends, hidden away and yet he never sees them, and is that my fault? Is it because of me? Do I hold him back to myself or is he ashamed of bringing them here?

We must get a new place, I cannot live any longer like this, out of his pocket. Yet how can I ask him to move? He says, 'Don't be ridiculous, it's yours as well as mine, now, that's all.' But not so.

Friday

I have written a longish poem (two pages) called 'Comminations'. It should begin the new volume which will come after 'Janus'. But I have lost several poems I had written, or thought that I had : perhaps they were only written in my head? Or else they have been taken away from me.

This morning a child was knocked down by a motor car in the street below, I looked out and saw the blood spouting up like a fountain from its chest as though it had been speared. And there was a woman, the mother I suppose, beating the car driver about the head. But then she began crying and trying to ask his forgiveness, and to forgive him, and they stood, two strangers before these few moments, and put their arms round one another and wept together, each was comforting the other. While

94

the child lay very still. It seemed not to be suffering at all. The ambulance was a long time.

Human beings are so rarely brought up against one another like that and give way to the truth at once, in this case, to mutual compassion.

Monday

We are going to the opera. Five times, three nights in a row and a break and then two nights, to *Eugene Onegin*, *The Magic Flute*, *Falstaff*, *Aida*, *Figaro*. So I have been down to Jermyn Street and bought an opera cloak lined with passion-purple silk. H. says I am very vain. I look very fine in it. I *am* vain. I am very happy. The cars roll down Piccadilly like chariots.

Friday

I want to sing myself, coming out of the opera house, to stand among the smells of russet apples and grapes and tangerines. The air is very cold, almost frosty. We walk back home. Everything is perfect. Nothing can ever go wrong again. 'Janus' is a good poem. I have something else to begin, a piece about Josh, the Meads' boy, and also a strange, cold-hearted piece which came into my head last night, to my surprise, about when Prentice struck his batman across the face the morning of the first Somme battle. The cruellest thing I saw in all the war. I am reading de Musset but he cloys. I shall go back to Baudelaire. Now H. brings me coffee and a glass of whisky liqueur, I shall go and sit with him.

I am very happy, my head is reeling with it, I have never before felt this teeming, seething joy in everything.

*

'We're going,' Francis said. 'We're moving, look, we really are!'

And it was true, the gap was widening gradually between boat and quay, there was a wedge of murky, oily water.

'We're *going*.'

He was leaning against the window, craning his neck. I had never seen anyone so excited, except a small child. But so often he was like that. He said, 'I hardly slept at all last night, I kept imagining everything, I went over the whole journey in my head. The way everything abroad tastes and smells quite different, the way the colour of the soil is so unlike our own boring old soil. I can't believe that we really are on the boat.' He was laughing, with delight and relief and enthusiasm, everything pleased him. He thought the seats the most comfortable in the world, the sailors the most handsome, the barman the most obliging, the passengers the most amiable. The drinks, he said, tasted entirely different from those you got on land. He made me explore the whole of the boat with him, we climbed up into the second class lounges and then further, on to the deck, and although it was squally and cold, the clouds swirling about the sky, he insisted that we should stand there for a long while, breathing in lungfuls of cold air, it would do us so much *good* he said, make new men of us. And then we walked from end to end, watching the Dover cliffs recede, going not paler but darker as we left them behind, and then moving ahead, we stared towards the French coast. But we could see nothing of it through the spray and mist. The boat was beginning to dip and roll more strongly as we got out into the open sea. Francis, who had never been seasick in his life and loved the rocking, pitching motion, wanted us to stay up there all the way. 'We won't get wet, we can pull our coats over our heads and sit in these deck-chairs, Harvey, it will be so much more *fun*.'

'You can. I'm going downstairs to have a drink and read a newspaper. I want to stay warm.'

'Oh well, if you like, if you must be *dull*. You are an old stick, sometimes anyone would think you were ninety-four.'

'I'm not stopping you from sitting up on deck all the way.'

'Of course you are, you know I shouldn't enjoy myself if you were skulking and sulking below.'

'I don't sulk.'

'Ah, it's too good a day to argue, it's the best day in the world. Look at us, setting off for Venice, nothing in our way – who is as lucky as we are, tell me that?'

And he bounded down the steps, almost landing in a heap at the bottom. I could not help responding to his mood, nor did I want to dampen his spirits, it made me happy to see him. And it worried me. I had watched this before, this elation, these moods of irrepressible euphoria, and where had they led?

'Don't look so glum.' He chinked his glass against mine. 'What on earth is wrong? Don't look at me like that.'

'Nothing's wrong at all.'

'No it isn't, is it? It absolutely is not.'

I put out a hand to prevent myself from lurching sideways off my chair as the boat rolled, but Francis was quite unperturbed, he swayed gently with the motion of the sea as he walked across to refill our glasses, he had learned the gait of the sailors.

'I went to Venice the first time when I was seven,' he said. 'They showed me pictures of it first. I didn't think all that water would appeal to me too much and then they told me I couldn't even swim or fish in it, so what would there be to *do*? Oh, I didn't like the sound of the place at all.'

'But you loved it.'

'No, of course not, I hated it, who wouldn't at seven? I was trailed about blazing-hot, hard pavements all day and taken into hundreds of churches dark as tombs and smelling of incense which made me feel sick. I was stood in front of enormous canvases as high as houses, the most tedious pictures of doges and madonnas and none of them laughing or even smiling, and they told me these were the most beautiful works of art in the world. I had to sit for hours on a hard iron café chair while they drank and talked, and talked and drank. We went to tea with a very old Contessa and had to wear velvet and a collar like a steel trap and bow and not say boo to a goose. Everything was so dark and the canals smelled and the Italian children gabbled in another language, I hated it. But I never forgot it. Children should have a large measure of the grotesque in their lives. I never forgot what it had been like to sail between those looming, decaying houses. It was like a magic city. But black magic. When I got home I drew pictures of it. I made them all brown and depressed-looking. I had nightmares about Venice. About being chased down alley ways by black cats and gargoyles with grinning faces. It's like Grimm's fairy tales – they terrify you and inspire you forever, they are part of the landscape of your imagination until you die.'

'Was there nothing at all you liked?'

'Oh, yes. The train journey there and the hotel page who

gave me rides in the lift and bits of old chocolate out of his trouser pockets.'

He had been talking at a furious rate, laughing, grimacing, waving his hands about, his eyes shining. Calm down, I wanted to say, you'll tip over the edge, you know where this will lead. I felt like an old nanny, predicting tears before bedtime, but I had seen them, I had seen them.

When we got into the sleeping car on the train at Calais, Francis spread out his arms and touched the bunk on one side and the wall on the other. 'Oh, it's smaller than ever, or else I've grown taller, I shall have to take the top bunk, I'm almost there already.' Then he turned to me, his face brilliant with pleasure. 'This is the best part, you know. In the train on the way. This is the best place in the world. Shall we simply stay on the train forever? We should arrive in Constantinople eventually. Harvey, we are free, we can go anywhere, do you realize that?' He sat down abruptly and shook his head as though he were dazed.

I wanted to enjoy this journey, too. I wanted to reach Venice. But I was tense, I spent the whole time glancing at him covertly, dreading a sudden blackening of his mood, or else some hysterical action. I could not relax.

It was already dark at Calais. We ate dinner in the mahogany and red plush dining car, on either side of a little lamp with a pleated silk shade. Francis said, 'This is the most perfect way to eat. This is the best dinner I have ever had in my life.'

It was good, certainly, and we drank a bottle of claret and then brandy, and swayed as the train swayed, back to the wagon-lit and the tightly made beds. Francis began to sing, bits from *The Magic Flute* and then the French aria from *Onegin*. He had a pleasant enough, quite tuneful tenor, but after a while, I suggested mildly that he might be disturbing others.

'Oh, for God's sake, Harvey, what's wrong with you? Why do you have to be such a kill-joy, why do you have to spoil every pleasure I ever have? Aren't things generally bad enough, don't you understand anything at all about me? I was happy, I was ... I wish I was going by myself, I wish I had never had anything to do with you.'

He had raised his voice almost to a shriek, so that the wagon-lit attendant had to tap on the door twice to ask what time we wanted to be called in the morning. I went hot with embarrassment.

'What time?' I asked Francis.

'Oh, I don't care, any damn time, what the hell does it matter?'

I opened the door slightly. 'Huit heures, s'il vous plaît.'

'Huit heures, merci, Monsieur. Dormez bien.' He was a fat man with a moustache. He gave me a hostile look while he spoke so courteously.

Francis was sitting on the top bunk. He said, 'What will happen to us?'

'We shall get a decent night's sleep.'

'It's important, Harvey. It may not be so to you, you may have a different view of the world. How do I know what you think?'

'You should by now.'

'What do other people think of me? What do they say?'

'People like you or dislike you, the same as any other man.'

'No. They talk to you, I know, you hear their opinions, don't you? You don't tell me but I know. Well, what do they say about me? That I am a madman and a time-waster and a drain on you. That's what they say. All those people. All *your* friends. They've no time for me.'

'That isn't true.'

'Stop pottering about and rummaging in your bags, look at me. I have to know about it.'

'For God's sake, Francis, will you stop shouting? I can hear you perfectly well but there's no reason why the rest of the train should do so.'

'You do like getting the upper hand, don't you? You like telling me what to do. You're my brother and the Head of School, you're one of them. I'm only here to be ordered about, isn't that it?'

'You know it is not.'

The train roared suddenly, going into a tunnel, so that I missed his next few words. When it was quieter I turned back to him and saw that he was lying down.

'He died, you know, the old boy who spoke all that poetry to me – Horatio. He died. Did I tell you?'

'Yes.'

'They put screens around him and I lay and heard him dying. The doctor came and shouted in his ear. "Can you hear me, Mr Beddoes? Can you hear me?" Then they started to talk about him over his bed. "It'll take some time. These old ones are always the slowest to go." How did they know that he couldn't hear them? How *dare* they talk about him as if he were an animal, already dead. I could have killed them.'

I had got into my bunk and dimmed the lights. I heard Francis turn, his voice came down to me, muffled and angry.

'It's all wrong, I tell you.'

'What is?'

'It's all wrong.'

'Francis, try and go to sleep.'

'All right.'

But I lay awake for a long time, hearing the juddering rhythm of the train and the air whistling past, smelling the smoke which streamed backwards and filtered in to us when we passed into a tunnel. Francis was quite still. Once I spoke to him quietly. There was no reply. In the end, I slept, but fitfully, chased by peculiar dreams.

When I woke, we were at a station somewhere. It was quite dark. The train was steaming like a blown-out horse.

'Harvey?'

'Hello?'

'Can we go back?'

I was silent, uncertain quite what he meant.

'Can we get off somewhere in the morning? As soon as possible. Can we just take a train back?'

'But why?'

'I don't want to go.'

'To Venice?'

'Yes. Or anywhere. But most of all to Venice. I'm afraid of what will happen to me there. I'm afraid of what it will be like.'

'But you know what it's like.'

'It traps you, Harvey . . . those houses . . . it's a terrible place.

All those graves on an island and they keep mad people on an island, too, they can never get away. What if they haven't learned to swim? And nothing but graves all over.'

'We don't have to go out there.'

'I want to go home. *Please*.'

I said, 'Whatever seems best to you.'

But if he replied, I did not hear him, I slept at once and heavily and dreamed no dreams.

Francis was shaking me. The compartment was filled with lemon-coloured sunlight. 'Look, look, wake up and look.'

We had stopped at one of the tiny village stations at the foot of the Alps. The early sun was streaming down through an almost transparent cloud cap, so that the vines on the lower slopes were in stripes of light and shadow. On the upper slopes of the granite-grey mountain, there was a little snow and a waterfall cascading down the left side into a valley of pine trees, tumbling and foaming, flecked with silver.

'I could stay here.' Francis said, 'I could live here, in one of those houses up the slope, right out of everybody's way. Think of it in winter.'

I did. Francis laughed. 'But I wanted you to see it.'

'What time is it?'

'Half past seven.'

I went back and lay on my bunk again and watched the blue sky and the puffs of cloud and the mountains slip past the window.

'If you want to go back,' I said, 'I think we could change at Montreux. We shouldn't be far away from there.'

'Go back? Go back where?'

He stared at me, wide-eyed. He knew. But he did not want me to remember. I waved my hand. 'Nothing.'

'We're going to *Venice*.' He sat on my legs, watching out of the window with me.

For the rest of the journey he was quieter. But when we curved around Lake Maggiore and into Stresa, he said, 'This is where we'll come, too, perhaps we could stop here on the way back? Oh, there are so many places I want to stay in.'

I dozed off just after Milan but Francis saw every field, every red-roofed farmhouse, every horse and cart and labourer, he was simmering with anticipation again.

We got our bags together and then stood in the corridor as the train crossed the flat marshland leading to Venice. It was like Suffolk, with the still mirrors of water on either side and the sea shimmering beyond, and nothing to interrupt the stretch of land and lake and sky except reeds and a single boatman, far in the distance, quite motionless. Francis was tense, his face pale, he was gripping my arm.

'Shall we be happy here?'

'Yes. Why not?'

'Will I be all right?'

I wanted to reassure him, I wanted him to go on looking forward. I could not. I did not know.

He turned his head away from me as the train began to slow down, coming into the station.

*

That first night in Venice we walked, I scarcely knew where or for how long, I became confused, because of Francis's mood and the amount we had to drink. I was tired when we arrived, I wanted to settle into the flat, have an early meal and go to bed. But Francis was wide-awake, his eyes swerving from side to side as we walked through the courtyard leading to the house, though I think that in fact he was actually seeing very little, he was restless, almost hysterical, receiving a million impressions at once. Venice had always made me lethargic and faintly low-spirited, but it brought Francis awake like a shot of adrenalin, he could not stop talking, could not wait to drop our bags and drag me out again into the town.

It was dusk, by the time we got up into the sitting-room, the sky had been the colour of blackberries over San Giorgio. The flat belonged to a cousin of my father who, when old age came upon him, had fled to the comforts of England and family. He had been a true Victorian, and these rooms expressed that peculiarly English-Venetian way of life. They were high-ceilinged and gloomy, with massive, ornate and rather shabby furniture and too much plush curtaining. I found them oppressive. Only one window, at the end of the sitting-room had a view, down towards the opening between the last houses, beyond which lay the Grand Canal. We could only see lights now, from gondolas and the vaporetti crossing towards the opposite bank, and from a palazzo, whose shutters had not yet been drawn, so that chandeliers shone out from every floor.

It was never possible to predict Francis's reaction to a place and I felt fearful, climbing the stone staircase, remembering how sombre the rooms were, wondering how greatly they might depress him.

'Candles,' he said at once, pivoting round. 'That's what we must have, straightaway – now – tomorrow – hundreds of candles, we must make it like a church.' He went to the window. There was another tall, shadowy building looming towards us across the narrow canal.

'It's unbelievable,' he kept saying, 'it's simply unbelievable.'

From the bedroom there was a vertiginous drop down into the cobbled courtyard below. The beds were very high, with elaborate brass fittings and goose-feather mattresses, the shutters were creaking, and painted with pale green and gold cherubims.

I said anxiously, 'It's a good deal lighter than this of course, in the daytime.'

'Oh, but I don't want that, we shall keep the shutters closed all the time, all day long, we must keep out the sun. It's so marvellous like this, don't you see? This is how you ought to live in Venice, we shall sit by candlelight all day. No, we can't have any sun.'

My heart sank, though he was not depressed, he spoke in a rush, full of plans, full of anticipation.

'Come on, come on, leave all this, we have to go out now, Harvey, we're in *Venice*, we have to go out into the streets. Come on.'

He began to throw things out of his suitcase, then turned to open another, then abandoned both and began to change his shoes and shirt.

'Come *on*.'

'Francis . . .'

'Oh, now what, what do you want?'

'Food, principally.'

He spread his arms out. 'Of course, my dear, we shall have food, we shall drink, we shall have everything – and music and people, and we'll walk, we'll go everywhere, it's like a carnival, it's just the beginning of everything.'

I went into the bathroom, which was panelled in mahogany, and had a bath standing on huge clawed feet.

'Harvey, what are you doing?'

'I'm grubby and travel-sore and so ought you to be.'

He came in and grabbed me by the arm, pulling me away from the taps, which had just begun to spout great gobbets of hot water.

'You don't want a bath, what on earth do you want a bath for, how dreary you are, there isn't time for baths now, we've got to go out.'

'Francis, we are here for weeks, not hours. It can all wait. Venice will still be there in the morning.'

'Don't you see I don't want it in the *morning*, who wants Venice in the morning? I shall sleep then, I shall sleep all day, it's the night, that's when you should go out here, it's all just beginning.'

I sighed, watching the bath-water empty again, and even when I insisted on rolling up my shirt-sleeves and scrubbing my hands and arms, Francis stood by dancing with impatience and irritation. He was flushed, he kept running his hands through his hair, he looked quite out of control – anyone seeing him would have been alarmed at once. I was terrified for him. And wondered, suddenly, why he wanted to be with me, conventional, cautious, perturbed as I was. I held him back, warned him about this or that danger, tried and always failed to keep up with his swiftly-changing moods. Now, I looked at him in amazement, seeing myself as he must see me. He was laughing. 'What on earth is the matter?'

I shook my head. I had asked myself as I lay awake in the train the previous night, whether I would honestly wish my life to be as it formerly was, whether I regretted meeting and loving Francis. He lay there in the bunk above my head, sleeping calmly. One moment he had been excited, the next full of dread, demanding to go back home. The past few months had been an appalling strain, full of misery, shock, apprehension, and the awful feeling of helplessness. What was to come? I knew that there was certainly worse. Could I cope? Should I have to give in? Did I wish to change things? Never mind how difficult it would be to leave, what scenes I should have to face, how guilty I should feel – was staying with him what I wanted?

Quite certainly, it was.

'Harvey, *please*.'

We went out. We began to walk through Venice.

It was quite dark now. There were only the lights, which so altered the face of the town, and yet at night Venice came into its own, there were shadows and tricks played by distance and water, it was an artificial place, not one of nature. Bright lozenges of light fell from the shop doorways on to the paving-stones. We went out of the Campo and turned left and then we began to hear all the footsteps sounding from every corner of the town, the voices which carried so far on the air. There were the smells of Venice, bread and toasting cheese, candle-grease, the reek of canals, cats, garbage and the sweet hair-oil of the men who passed us by.

Francis stopped in front of every shop-window, staring entranced at the shining, twisted shapes of glass, at fish and loaves and lace. He bought a little pastry of almonds and cherries, warm and crumbling in his hand. We went into a *Parfumeria* and I waited while he chose from among the dozens of bottles of toilet water, tipping out a little of each one on to his hand, consulting with the proprietor. Then he wanted to drink and to try everything, he could not make up his mind where to begin. We drank vermouth first, standing up at a counter among a group of workmen, and then moved on to an expensive café with tables on the pavements and an awning of gold and blue, and drank Martinis, and Aurum. It was a warm evening and I began to feel unsteady, the lights doubled and shifted about. But Francis had only just begun.

And so we went on with our feverish wandering, up and down narrow passages, over canals, in and out of squares and then over the Accademia bridge, below which the water shone raven-black and on through now silent and deserted streets towards the Zattere. Occasionally, a cat glided past us through the darkness, eyes gleaming. We heard only our own footsteps. I wanted to ask Francis what he was looking for, where we should end.

Out on the waterfront it was noisy again, the cafés were full, a piano accordion was playing somewhere. The lights from the Giudecca looked very far away, there seemed to be an endless expanse of water.

'No,' Francis said, at once. 'No, this is no good, this won't do, let's go back.'

We went back, passing innumerable restaurants at which I wanted to stop and eat, but Francis kept hold of my arm and pulled me on, towards the Rialto. Once, he stopped dead in the middle of a small, empty square. It was like reaching the end of a labyrinth. We heard a scream, then the sound of a man and woman quarrelling, shrieking and hissing at one another, the sound echoing down between the houses.

'I want to go on the boat now,' Francis said, and so we waited for the vaporetto, and sat right at the front, not under cover, and went zig-zagging from bank to bank all the way down the Grand Canal.

At San Marco I stood up. 'No,' said Francis, 'No, no.'

'Look, we're not going all the way to the Lido.'

'Well – just to the gardens then. Please.'

I sat down again. And was glad, then, that I had, suddenly I was no longer tired and it was beautiful, passing so slowly along the Schiavoni, seeing the lights strung up around the cafés. A party of sailors were walking in a long line, ten or twelve of them, arm in arm right across the pavement, their white suits making them look ghostly, and the ribbons streaming behind their hats like pigtails.

Then it went quiet again, there was only the chugging of the engine and the sound of the water turning and slapping beneath us. We were the only people left on the boat. When we got off at the Public Gardens, we stood, to watch them move away and out into the open lagoon, the lights blinking. A cat slithered against our legs and at once Francis bent down and began to fondle it. It was very small, very thin, with a soft grey face.

'Oh, I want to give it something, look at it, look how thin it is.'

'They're all thin. And we haven't got anything.'

'Oh, Harvey, I can't bear to leave it, what will it do? It will starve. *Look* at it.'

'They don't starve you know, they catch rats and mice, and a lot of people do bring them scraps.'

'Let's go back and get some food for it.'

'I'm rather hungry myself.'

The world was beginning to seem unreal and the sky tipped a little as I stood upright. But Francis was still on his knees stroking the cat, its purrs sounded like a sewing machine across the silent gardens.

'Now it will follow us, we'll never get rid of it.'

'I don't care if it does, we'll take it back with us. We'll keep it at the flat.'

'And when we leave?'

Another time he might have screamed abuse at me. Now he stood up.

'Yes,' he said, 'of course. Good-bye, cat.'

We walked on. The cat did not follow us, it vanished into the bushes. The air smelled differently here, of earth and bitter rhododendron leaves, and faintly of the sea. The trees were rustling slightly.

'I've done with all the noise now, I like it here best, I don't want any more noise. I shall come here every night.'

We sat down on a bench and looked out across the black lagoon.

'San Clemente,' I said, not thinking.

'What's there?'

I did not reply.

'Oh, I know, I know, the island of lunatics. How tactful you are, my dear, really, how you do try to protect me from the nastiness of life.'

'No.'

'Well, I wonder how full it is and whether they've room for another. How many people go mad in Venice, do you suppose? Hundreds and hundreds, I think, it's a place where all the people are mad. It doesn't exist, you see, except in a lot of fevered brains, it's a mirage, it's a peep-show, didn't you realize?'

'And also a city full of hard-headed bankers.'

Francis laughed shortly. 'You don't know,' he said. 'You don't know.'

The wind blew off the water, then, damp, tasting of winter. I stood up. 'Food,' I said firmly. 'Food and then bed.'

Francis smiled at me seraphically, his spectacles shining.

And we had food, eventually, an enormous meal of shellfish and veal in a tiny café off the Merceria. But then we went walking again. The shops had closed long ago, the grilles were up, lights out. There were fewer people in the streets. Only, here and there, the bars were smoky, and either quite deserted or very full. We went into half a dozen or more, drinking, drinking. I was quite drunk by now, following Francis, uncertain where we were or how we would get back to the flat. Then in the end the cafés closed too, it was one, two, three o'clock and still we were walking. We crossed the Piazza. Our footsteps rang. The chairs of Florian's and Quadri's were piled up like furniture waiting to be removed, and on all the ledges and crevices the pigeons huddled, sleeping. It was eery to walk across that great open square without having them scrambling about under one's feet.

We sat down on the steps of a drinking fountain in the middle of some other square. The moon had come out and fell upon the façade of a church and the terrible face of a gargoyle with an open black mouth. It was a cold, friendless moonlight, spreading peculiar shadows.

Francis was leaning against me. I thought he was asleep but when I shook my head to try and clear it, he moved, laughing softly.

'It's all wrong, I tell you.'

'What?'

'It's all wrong.'

'We'd better get up.'

'No.' He sounded quite sober, his voice was clear and quiet.

'Harvey – are you all right?'

'Just about. Tired.'

'Good.'

Then we heard it, from somewhere in the shadows on the

other side of the square, the shuffling footsteps and the low voice. Francis started. I understood a soft stream of obscenities. We were being spied upon and accused. I managed to stand up.

'Come along.'

He was sitting with his hands on his chin and I realized that he was crying, though quite silently and not moving. I bent down again. And again the whisper from the other side of the square. Someone spat.

'I can't stop it. I can't stop it.'

'It's all right, Francis, come on, get up. We don't have to go far.'

'You see, it doesn't matter what I try to do, it doesn't matter what game I play with it, I can't win. And it doesn't take bribes either. I can't sell my soul for it. It always comes back, it always will, won't it? You know that. You know.'

It was a long time before he could come with me, I don't think he heard what I was saying, he was wrapped up within himself, fighting the battle that raged inside his own head, knowing what was to come and dreading it. We went back through the alleys. Venice was a dark, lifeless, decaying place, there were no more lights, no creatures, no people except a voyeur hidden somewhere, the city seemed to have broken off from the rest of the living world and to be floating slowly away, there was to be no future here only a past, and all the buildings were dead as a row of teeth set in a skull.

I knew that we should never have come here. I knew it was the wrong place and things were going to be bad now, though I could not tell how bad or for how long. I felt like packing up at once, not sleeping at all but taking the first train out in the morning, back to the mainland and then – anywhere. But it was not up to me. It never would be.

We got to bed somehow and slept until well into the next afternoon, when the light came piercing here and there like needles between the shutters. Francis woke with a headache, his face was puffy. I looked down at him and he turned his head away from me on the pillow.

'Do get out, Harvey, do go and pack and leave while you can, do get away. I wish you would.'

'Do you?'

He clawed at the sheets and tried to push himself down, to suffocate in the pillows, as the storm of weeping broke over him. I made coffee and took it to him, dressed and sat in a chair by the bed. I had found hundreds of tall, tapering candles and now I lit a dozen of them and put them about the room. The shutters stayed tightly folded together all of that day.

But the cycle of Francis's madness was never a regular or predictable one. I had prepared myself for days, perhaps weeks, spent closeted in that dismal flat by candlelight, having to comfort and support him through his deepest apathy and depression. Certainly, for the next two days he stayed in bed or sat slouched in a chair looking as though he were half drugged, his eyes blank and all his attention turned inward upon himself. He hardly spoke to me and when he did answer a persistent question, it was with a monosyllable. He would not shave or eat or read, but only sat up once in a while and muttered to his own hands. 'It's all wrong, I tell you, it's all wrong.' Once I caught him staring at himself in a mirror, his face very close to the glass. He looked puzzled. 'I'm afraid we have not been introduced,' he said to his own reflection. 'I do not know your face. Should I know your face? Is this a good party?'

But on the third day he woke looking altered again, more like his calmer self, he began to get dressed, paying scrupulous attention to the set of his tie and cufflinks and the colour of his socks, polishing his shoes with great vigour.

'Harvey, I have to go out. Open the shutters. Is it raining?'

It was not. I could see the sun and the sky glazed-blue like a china plate above the roof-tops. I wanted to ask if he was sure he knew what he wanted, but was afraid of his reaction. And perhaps any desire for activity and a change of scene was better than the lethargy of the past two days.

We went out and he seemed entirely well. Venice wore a different complexion, it was full of sunlight, the terra-cotta and sand-coloured façades of the palazzi were softened by the rippling reflections from off the water, and, where they were painted, the gold lines were picked out and shone. It was as warm as June in the Campo where we sat drinking coffee and watching the children play. Francis began to scrutinize the

Venetians, they had, he said, the most rare and patrician beauty in the world, males and females alike, and then I saw them with new eyes, and he was right. Time and again he would nudge me and point out some tall slim Venetian with the high aristocratic nose and clear skin, the tawny, or red-gold hair. He would pick one and pursue him through the streets, enchanted with his slimness and the erect, aloof way he walked. I began to see the citizens of the city of the past all around us, to place the long superior faces of the older men, whom one could see, more elaborately dressed, in the procession of churchmen and doges painted by Guardi and Canaletto. They were always unsmiling, unlike the rest, the dark, short, plebeian Italians. We sat a few tables away from a young couple one afternoon, and Francis said they were a Prince and a Madonna out of a painting by Bellotto. I could believe him. They were very young, both astonishingly beautiful, and they sat rather apart from one another, and did not speak at all, as though conscious of being portraits within a frame.

That was a happy week. We got up late and ate long, leisurely lunches, we wandered through squares and sat about in the sun. Francis looked well, though he was oddly distant from me, as though he had some abstract problem on his mind. He took most pleasure either in sitting about or in riding from one end of the Grand Canal to the other on the vaporetto.

One morning he went out alone to be measured for a pair of hand-made boots. When he came back, just before one o'clock, he was not alone. I heard several pairs of footsteps on the stone stairs. He opened the sitting-room door and I saw some people behind him, standing huddled together. He asked me hurriedly how much money I had.

'Why?'

'Never *mind* – how much?'

I looked in my wallet. I had about eleven pounds.

'Oh, that's all right then. I was hoping – only you see I've just paid for my boots, I only had a couple of hundred lire and this family came up to me on the Accademia bridge – well, the woman and her child did, they were begging. But I really had so little money, and when I gave it to them I realized there was no point in that, it's easy enough to hand out coins, isn't it? But they're so poor, Harvey, and I made them take the money and then go and fetch the old grandfather they told me about – they said the money was for him, there isn't a husband, apparently. I don't quite understand. Anyway, they're here outside and I promised to take them for a decent meal and buy clothes for the child and shoes and ... well, you see, then I realized that I had no money. But if you've got eleven pounds then it's all perfectly all right. Let's go straightaway.'

The family were silent and suspicious. It would not have occurred to Francis that he might have made them feel profoundly uncomfortable by bringing them here, that he was not doing them a kindness.

'Look, give them this money, they'd much rather go out and buy food and things themselves, they don't want us with them.'

For it was certainly pointless to reprimand him, to explain that he could not give all we had to every beggar in Venice, that he would have despised utterly, though, another day, he might easily have passed by the woman on the bridge without noticing her at all, no matter how importunate she became.

'No, no, that won't do at all, that's just too easy and, besides, how do we know they won't go out and spend it all on drink and I want the child to have shoes and things. Oh, do come *on*.'

I went. It was the most bizarre and disconcerting afternoon I have ever spent. The family were obviously very poor indeed, their clothes were torn and patched, the woman wore old slippers, the man and child were grubby. They spoke no English and seemed reluctant to answer my remarks in Italian, though Francis chattered away to them and never noticed their failure to respond. He wanted to treat them lavishly, to take them somewhere grand to eat but I managed to persuade him how out of place that would make them feel, and we found a café near the vegetable market, where they ate more food than I have ever seen consumed at a single sitting – soup and pasta, roast veal, potatoes, salad, fruit, ice cream, cheese. The child stared at Francis throughout the meal, a knowing, worldly stare : her face was wizened, she looked weary, a hundred years old, she had never been young. She ate like an animal.

When they had finished, Francis was not satisfied, he would not hear of leaving them to buy their own clothing. Instead, we went trailing about the poorer shopping streets with them, fitting the child and the old man with shoes, the mother with a dress, a black cardigan, stockings, a shawl. I spent all the money I had brought with me and went to exchange more, so that we could buy cakes and ice cream for tea. Then Francis began to choose presents for them, toys for the child, sweets, bags of pastries, tobacco. He was excited, gay, full of enthusiasm. I was profoundly uncomfortable. The family were stolid, morose, accepting.

When we finally parted from them, I felt giddy, I wanted to rush away and hide my head. They walked off down a narrow street without turning to look back at us and I felt a mixture of shame and misery on their behalf, and perplexity and annoyance with Francis. I was silent, walking back to the house.

'No,' he said abruptly. 'No, I don't want to be there anymore for ages, let's go and look at the water.'

We were standing by the Colleoni statue and the sun was pouring down, trapped here by the high houses and the church.

'I'm worn out, Francis, I've had enough of your whims for one day.'

'But I had to see that they were all right, don't you understand? I couldn't just give them the money.'

'Oh, I suppose not.'

'Besides, what have we done? Bought them a meal and a few bits of this and that and how long will that last them, what difference has it really made to their lives?'

'We've done what we can.'

'Do you want to go home now?'

'I'd like a drink.'

The café tables were hot to the touch, the paint blistering in the sun. Yet to the Venetians it was October and therefore autumn, they frowned in disapproval at our shirt-sleeves. All the women wore heavy black with long sleeves and shawls.

We had a bottle of Orvieto, dry as lemons. Francis's hand had begun to shake a little as he held the glass. Then he noticed a chip of cork floating in the wine. Instead of getting it out, he snapped his fingers at the waiter and began to make a scene, to accuse him of slovenliness and demand a fresh bottle for which we would not pay. Finally, he poured the contents of his glass over the man's feet. No one took any notice of us at all. The waiter's face was wooden. The bottle was removed and a fresh one brought. Francis had a queer, frenzied look in his eyes and he drank the wine very quickly, downing glass after glass. Once, he turned to me. 'They've got to learn,' he said. 'And I'm here to teach them. It's all wrong, I tell you.'

I paid quickly and got him away. We had reached the Campo which led back towards our house, when a cat streaked across, almost tripping up a man a few yards away from us. In a gesture of impatience he lashed out with his foot, swearing, but although the cat had gone, and the kick went nowhere near it, Francis let out a bellow of rage and distress, and lunged towards the man, stood in his path and, before I could reach him, had struck out, his fist met the Italian's jaw with a sound that echoed like a bullet-shot across the afternoon quiet of the square. With the help of a couple of waiters from the café opposite I pulled Francis off and pinned his arms behind him, trying at the same time to explain as well as I could that he was ill, shocked and distressed, that he had not known what he was doing.

The Italian was wiping his face very delicately with a white handkerchief. He was a slight man, he looked as if his bones were brittle as a bird's, and yet he had not fallen and was not bleeding. I still held Francis tightly, but he was unresisting now, staring down at the cobbles and muttering something to himself.

'Signore . . .'

The man folded his handkerchief and replaced it in his pocket. Then he looked from Francis to me and back again. The waiters had retired to their tables but were intent, waiting for the fight to break out again. It was suddenly quite silent in the square, nothing moved, I looked down and saw our long, flat shadows lying across the sunlit cobbles and felt as though we were on a stage, and in all the windows around us people were sitting, as in the boxes of a theatre, watching, nodding, waiting to hiss or to applaud.

I tried to apologize. The Italian stopped me. He said one word, 'Madman', and spat into Francis's face. Then he turned and walked off with great dignity, very straight-backed, out of the square.

The cat had emerged again, it sat beside a stone lion outside one of the doors, eyes half-closed, inscrutable, a sleek, domestic beast.

Both waiters were leaning insolently against the wall, still watching us. I led Francis away.

For the next fifteen days he was completely demented. He did not know me. He did not know where he was. He muttered under his breath and occasionally shouted out, but nothing he said made any sense and always he returned to the same phrase, 'It's all wrong I tell you, it's all wrong.' I told the maid and the caretaker that he had an infectious illness, so that they would keep away from the flat, and when he was sleeping I went out to buy food for us and raced back, terrified at what I might find. At night, I dozed in an armchair, for he had taken to getting up and lighting candles, and setting fire to paper spills, watching the flame creep down them and then dropping the last few smouldering inches on to the floor. Sometimes he sat for three or four hours at a time with his head in his hands, leaning on the table. Sometimes he laughed maniacally, frightening me, other times he wept and then roared with distress. He began to beat his fists upon the walls, and sometimes his head, so that I had always to be alert, ready to restrain him. And then he would go for me, flailing out and butting me in the chest. I was exhausted, scarcely eating anything myself, strained beyond what seemed endurable. I wondered how long I could go on with this, and certainly I wished profoundly that we had never come abroad, for if I had to give in and get medical help, it would be much less complicated at home.

Then one Sunday morning, when we had been in Venice for three weeks, he again asked to go out. He seemed to know me, and went searching for the cupboard which held his clothes – though it was the wrong cupboard in the wrong room. I had the greatest possible misgivings after the episode in the square, I was afraid he would break away from me and disappear down the maze of alleys. Anything might happen then. I began to imagine him in a Venetian prison or hospital, or on the island of lunatics.

But we went and he walked quite calmly, though in a strange, uncertain way, as though he could not exactly co-ordinate his limbs. We went a long distance and came out eventually on to the Fondamente Nuove. The wind was blowing quite hard across the water, which was choppy, flecked here and there with white. It was cold, even in the sun. We passed the marble monument shops and the flower stalls, mingling with the Venetian families, all dressed in their best, dark, formal clothes. When Francis saw the boat for which they were silently queueing, carrying their flowers and gripping their children by the hand, he went towards it at once and, because I was afraid to cross him in anything, I went too, we shuffled slowly forwards until we got on board, and it was packed, full of those respectful, preoccupied mourners.

San Michele was beautiful and quite silent, after the boat had left, apart from the sound of footsteps. We walked for a long time up and down between the gravestones. The sky was faintly misty, an opalescent blue-grey, and the slabs of white marble and black granite threw no shadows. Francis seemed very tranquil, very soothed, he hummed a little under his breath as we walked. Once, we saw a woman kneeling to arrange a pot of butter-yellow chrysanthemums and weeping, weeping. Francis stared at her and I was afraid that he might begin to weep himself. But he moved on, we turned down another aisle of graves.

He would not leave for a long time, though it was even colder, here, the wind cut across from the open sea, blowing at the flowers and the black veils of the women. Then, the sun went in altogether, the fog had risen, like ectoplasm between the cypress trees. I touched Francis's arm.

'Yes,' he said, and smiled at me suddenly, an open, loving smile.

We went back in silence on the boat and walked home in silence too, but it was not an oppressive, stricken silence. He had turned some corner, there was some lightening of the terrible pressure inside his head.

*

Monday

Venice, Venice, how I detest you, how could I ever have thought you were beautiful, how could I have wanted to come here, how did I believe in any of it? Now I see the death which is everywhere. The beggar child had been dead for a thousand years, she was one of those old, old royal infantas in a painting, ugly, full of the knowledge of evil and a dull yearning for oblivion.

Tuesday

It is so hard to work. I must write, anything to try and clear my head. Nothing matters today. The fog has come, it rains all day, splattering into the canals. It is grey, the bases of all the houses are slimed yellow-green with weed, all the pillars are rotting and crumbling away. And the water too, that is filthy, it is swill, garbage floats past, there is a film of oil on the surface. There is no freshness here, nothing is new or young, there is no fresh flowing of blood. The veins are dried up and cracked and lead nowhere but back upon themselves. But I like these rooms, they are dark, grandiose things, those who lived here must have pretended to be Counts, they had a gondola mooring, but perhaps never their own gondola.

And all the gondolas are black.

Wednesday

We must leave here, there is the terrible rottenness in the air and now it is cold, too, it is winter and the lights are no longer shining out, the surface of the piazza is greased over with damp and the feathers of the pigeons moult in the rain. What is there to do here? There is nothing to do. I cannot work. I have tried again. Oh, and I was going to write a set of poems, they were to be about the grace and elegance and timelessness of this place, with its face mirrored in the waters – the way it floats like an enchanted castle on a lake of glass: there were to be people hooded and masked, laughing, interchangeable, pursuing one another down the secret passages of the city and I still see them, I see them everywhere, their eyes stare out at me, burning within their skulls, but they are dead and there is nothing I have to say about them. It is a dance of death. So I cannot work.

My head feels very light, very empty, I am floating about in this world and too tired to move and too bitter about this place to stay in it. I lie in bed. I want to be in England. Or in the mountains. In any small, anonymous place, a working, living place, full of growing things. For here nothing grows, there is nothing made by God.

Thursday

I have not written in this journal before now, since we came here and I expected to write every day, it would be full, singing with all the ideas and things we had seen.

But I have seen nothing.

I think H. is unhappy but he has been reading a lot. He buys figs and fennel and marvellous fish for us to eat, red mullet and eels and huge fat crabs. Yet he is not working either and sometimes I see his face and it is an old face, worn and bewildered and that is my fault, he has given up too much for me.

*

'Harvey, we must leave tomorrow, I can't stay here, tomorrow we are going home. And when I get home I shall go into hospital.'

He stood, leaning against the great carved fireplace, smiling a little. It was early in the morning.

'Are you feeling ill?'

'You know what I mean.'

Yet for the past few days, ever since our visit to San Michele, he had been coming out slowly from under the last cloud and today he looked himself again.

'You see, it can't possibly go on like this. I am simply dragging you down and I'm not being fair to myself either. Perhaps there are things they can do for me and they will make me well, Harvey, forever and ever.'

I put aside my book. He meant it, for now, for the moment: he always committed himself entirely to whatever mood he happened to be in.

'I've been having a good talk to myself, you see, trying to teach myself a thing or two. I've been hiding behind you, I've ... Well, but that's no good and it's all over and done with and I shall get them to cure me. I shall be looked after and then I shall be well and we can be happy, I shall be able to work, things will go right with us.'

'Things are right with us now, you know.'

'While you are the nurse and the asylum keeper and the cook and the policeman and have no life or work of your own and I cause you nothing but worry? I am the most selfish, evil, despicable man, haven't you realized that? But it doesn't matter, because I have. I have seen it.'

He went on and on, dramatizing himself, being expansive, blaming himself, full of plans for the future.

'So we must go. I can't stay here any longer. I cannot bear this place.'

Nor could I. I had come to hate Venice. I felt imprisoned and now that the days were so bleak and fog-bound and damp, it was even worse. We only went out to drink in half-empty bars and then tramp back to the flat through the rain. We had to have the lights on all day and even then my eyes were strained trying to read. I had also missed most of all the presence of friends, the chance of meeting them in a street, the brief exchanges of pleasantries. Both Francis and I spoke passable Italian but we were strangers in this city, the faces of its inhabitants and the doors of its dark houses were closed to us, though perhaps if he had not been ill for those weeks, we might have taken up the few introductions we had to the English people living in Venice. As it was, we saw no one except the caretaker and the maid, waiters and shop-keepers. We spoke only to one another, we were relying upon one another, draining our mutual resources of affection and companionship as never before. I looked around the room now, at the leather-bound books in their tall glass cases, at the heavy candelabra, and the tapestries. How had we borne it for so long?

'Yes,' I said, and got up at once, anxious to see to the packing, buy our tickets, to feel that I was on the way home. 'Yes, you're right about leaving. "Janus" will be out. We can't stay on abroad.'

'But I shall go somewhere for treatment, I shall ring their bells and rattle at their gates and you must come with me, you must tell them what happens, they have got to help me, they must let me in.'

I did not reply. I thought he almost certainly had no idea what he was really saying.

Two days later, we were getting off the vaporetto at the railway station. It was a raw, dark day. As our train pulled out I looked back and could see nothing at all of the city, the whole lagoon was shrouded in fog, the island might not have existed.

'Oh, God,' Francis leaned his head against the cold window-pane. 'Oh, thank God. I feel like a man escaping from prison. That's what we've done, do you realize? We had buried our-selves, we were like your Egyptians, Harvey, because that's what Venice is, a giant mausoleum, full of precious, dead things, meaningless treasures. You don't breathe air, you breathe dust and death, you suffocate. But you look about you and see the things that shine here and there, the silver and the gold, and they deceive you, you think they are alive and you are alive, you walk and talk and all the time you are bound in burial clothes and the exits are all sealed.'

'Then we've broken them down.'

We were passing through the fields outside Padua. Like Francis, I was light-headed with relief.

'I know how Lazarus felt. Oh, when we get home, I shall work and work, it's all buzzing about in my head now. I shall write some poems about Dorset first, about barrows and badgers, but there's something else much more important.' He leaned forward. He almost never talked to me about his work. 'You see, the world spins and turns on its axis and there is light on one side and darkness on the other, life here and death there and, at the very darkest point, the innermost heart of the dark-ness, there is the seed of the light, and when the light is the brightest, then at that point, darkness has already begun. You see, it's all inside one's own head, too, inside my head, I can feel it. It's what the Elizabethans knew about the microcosm, but I have to try and say it all so clearly that everyone will see, there's no good my playing tricks and being clever with people, the world isn't like that, not really, though it seems to be. But being isn't seeming. This truth is all contained in the most pre-cise and perfect form, like Kepler's snowflake, and the form must never obscure what is within it but if the form isn't there, everything falls into chaos and there is nothing, oh, it's all ... But now I know where to begin. I think. It sounds ... But I shall have to work and work at finding the form and saying it all in the right order, not muddling things up. I must begin, I must start as soon as we get home. I know what I want to do.'

I had never heard him think aloud in this way and I thought he sounded confused. But nearly three years later, when the long poem called 'Earth, Air, Water, Fire' was finished, I saw embedded at the heart of it everything that he had been trying to express that day in the train. Though of course, then, he was still stumbling about. In the poem he formulated his thoughts and matched them to particular observations, gave them metaphor, worked them out as carefully as a philosopher, or a scientist constructing theorems. But it was not science or philosophy, he wrote it as poetry, and the words sang and danced across the pages, he had never before achieved such command of language. It was a very different poem from 'Janus', superficially much more simple and lyrical, yet essentially deeper, more important, the work of a mind which was finally coming to an understanding of the world and of itself.

But understanding was not control. If Francis knew what he was, he could not alter it, he had no power at all over the vagaries and eruptions of his own mind. He was helpless in the face of an attack of insanity, no matter which way it went with him, whether he was depressed or violent, whether he was hysterical, agitated or deluded by visions and voices.

We arrived back in London nine days before Christmas, and at once he began to work. He had mentioned to me several times that he was not entirely happy in Sackville Street, because the flat was 'mine'. So now I began to look for another home, in which he would feel at ease. I found it on Christmas Eve, and we shared the purchase of it. Francis approved, but I think he would have agreed to anything just then, he was entirely absorbed in the new poem, knowing that he might not remain well and in control of his work for very long, that he had to make use of every moment.

The house was a three-storeyed one in South Terrace. I thought that we should be better away from the racket of Piccadilly and nearer to Kensington Gardens which I so much liked. We had a first floor sitting-room running the whole length of the house, with tall windows at each end and a balcony. At the back, between high brick walls, was a small beautiful garden planted with old climbing roses, mignonette and Albertine, wistaria and clematis and large azalea bushes. Francis liked all of it, and liked also the two bay trees standing on either side of the front door, under which, he said, the wicked would surely flourish.

We moved in on January 2. Eight days later, 'Janus' was published.

Then it all began. I have the files of reviews here on my desk, from the literary journals and academic magazines, from the daily and weekly newspapers. The articles vary from a hundred to over a thousand words in length and they are dated mostly between January and May of that year.

How often is a poem, especially a long, difficult poem, not readily accessible to the general reader, so immediately accepted and lauded and even understood?

It is much more usual for a poet to have to wait ten, twenty, fifty years for his best and most influential work to be acknowledged. I think Francis suspected not only that this was so, but that it ought to be so, that instant success would be a detrimental thing for him.

He was not, of course, an unknown writer. His war poetry and the few youthful pieces which preceded them had gained recognition, he had been called 'rising', 'promising', 'fresh'. But now he was acclaimed as a major artist.

'Well, it means that they'll listen to me again,' he said, after reading one of the longer, more scholarly reviews. 'It means I shan't have to fight round after round. But look at what I have to live up to now, look what they will expect from me and how glad they'll be to do me down.'

Apparently, that was more or less all he felt. The detailed critical analyses of 'Janus' sometimes irritated but more often amused him. Even those who praised him the most extravagantly had sometimes 'no idea', they thought they understood him but they did not; they either read into the poem much that was not there, or else missed much that was. But Francis never, so far as I remember, adopted that blasé and uncharitable attitude towards his admirers, even towards those who might have been only sycophants, too eager to jump upon his bandwagon for the furtherance of their own ends.

'It's kind of them to like me,' he said, 'they mean so well, Harvey, don't they?'

If within a few weeks he had become an eminent poet, it only served to make him work all the more painstakingly. There were days when he wrote only four or five lines, others when he produced thirty in half the time. He knew precisely where he was going and yet he seemed to be groping his way there step by step. He got up very early and brewed coffee and then went up to his room at the top of the house, looking down on to the garden. He had made himself a sort of eyrie, between high piles of books. He had begun to collect early scientific instruments, compasses, sextants, an armillary sphere, and on the walls were charts made by the early astronomers and global navigators. He was always going out and buying some object which intrigued him; he had an hour-glass, a small stuffed kingfisher under a dome, two silver lockets containing coils of hair, apothecary's jars and chunks of amber, rose and blue quartz, marble, coral and cornelian.

He burned candles constantly even though it was a light room, so that there was always a faint tallow smell hovering about the top landing.

Once, he had told me that he could never work seriously in London because of his inability to refuse invitations, and the lure of shops and theatres. But now he went out socially very little, only walked in the afternoons up towards Hyde Park or down into Chelsea and along the embankment. He would not answer the telephone, he declined all the invitations from his former circle and he rebuffed, often rather rudely, the advances made by fellow poets and writers, even from the eminent.

'I've got to get on, Harvey, I must not waste time, I'm quite happy as I am, I don't want to go out anywhere.'

And so I wrote the notes of apology and covered up for him when I could. My monograph was almost finished, and I had begun to think of writing a much longer one, on the great temple at Karnak.

We lived an orderly, industrious life at South Terrace. To-wards the end of April when it began to be warmer, Francis took a table down into the garden and worked there. I would look down at him sometimes from the sitting-room and see his head bent low, almost touching the paper, or else notice that he had gone over to stare into the roses, the words weaving about in his head. Often he sat for an hour or more without writing anything at all, often he went upstairs to consult a book, or else out through the front door, to walk, perhaps for ten minutes, perhaps for two hours.

I relaxed. He was well. 'Janus' began to attract attention in America now. Francis said it all seemed very far away to him, it might have been written by someone else, he was so involved with the new piece.

Two years passed. Two years. It is hard to remember how long a time that really was for him to be well and yet how short it seemed to be. We went abroad twice, to Provence and then for six weeks to a remote Greek island, Skiathos, where the hundreds of small screech-owls had, Francis thought, the most evil faces in the whole natural world. But never again to Venice. My first monograph was published, and well enough received in a quiet, backwater way, by my fellow scholars. To celebrate it, Francis bought me an exquisite small watercolour by Whistler. I have it here in my study now, I look at it constantly, it is the most beautiful thing I have ever owned.

In those days, Francis was quite often asked to gatherings in Bloomsbury. He always refused, or else I refused for him, but I think that although that circle was rather piqued they never did him any unkindness, their public comments upon his work were always perceptive and generous.

'Ah, but you don't know what they say about me when they get their heads together, my dear.' He laughed, enjoying the thought of it, making up the scenes in his mind. And then went on working, working.

They ask me what is the strongest impression I still retain of him, and I say industry, industry and patience. He did not miss a day at work during those years, and when he was not writing, he was reading, he went through the French and German philosophers as well as poets and novelists, he read sixteenth-century metaphysicians and astronomers and explorers, he read St Augustine and Marcus Aurelius, he read Hobbes and Kant, John Dee, Coleridge, Hume, Berkeley, Locke, Butler. He translated many of Chaucer's immediate predecessors and contemporaries into modern English – at that time many of them were scarcely known, outside the universities.

The only relaxation he allowed himself – for on his walks he was always thinking about work – was visiting the galleries. He once made a list of the pictures he would be most likely to try and steal: they included anything by Turner and Stubbs, and William Dyce's 'Pegwell Bay, Kent: A Recollection', in the Tate Gallery. I do not know why he had such a devotion to this painting. It must have struck some chord of early memory for him, for I am sure that his response to it was more than purely visual. 'But they don't look at it,' he would say. 'No one bothers about it, they can't see what it's about.'

He felt at the same time profoundly in tune with his own times and yet hostile to them, too, artists so often seemed to him to skate over the mirror of truth, dazzled by its shining surface and by their own reflections in it.

I do not go to London now. I try to remember it as it was then. When I look at the covers of 'Comminations' and 'Earth, Air, Water, Fire' I see the house in South Terrace, I am inside that treasure-filled, candle-lit room where Francis worked. I do not want to imagine any of it as it may now be.

Two years and four months. I have written it down in my diary. For all of that time, Francis was well.

When the blow fell it was late May and warm, the roses were out. He had gone for a walk immediately after lunch. By six o'clock he had not returned. It was still evening and in any case the garden of the house was always quiet: a blackbird was singing on a fence a dozen houses away and all the notes came to me clear and full and confident on the air. I was sitting in one of the cane chairs reading a newspaper, wanting a drink, wondering when Francis would reappear. I had got out of the habit of worrying about him. There was no need, no need.

The telephone rang.

*

He had been carrying a letter in his pocket, addressed to South

Terrace. But by the time the police telephoned me he had already been admitted to a mental hospital in Battersea.

'Are you the next of kin, Mr Lawson?'

'No.'

'A relative?'

'A friend. We share a house.'

'Would you have the address of his next of kin?'

'There's no use your getting in touch with them, he never sees them, they have nothing to do with him at all.'

'They *are* the next of kin, sir.'

'This is what they've been *wanting* to happen to him.' I had raised my voice and heard the echo of it in the small office. 'I beg your pardon.' I gave him the address and as I did so, I felt more ashamed than I had ever felt, more guilty of betraying him. I knew what his family would say, and what he would think of them, too. 'I must go and see him. I must go at once.'

But I lingered, wanting to be told what had happened, to try and understand.

By the time his behaviour had been brought to the attention of the police, it was late in the afternoon. But they had seen him earlier, the strollers and the park keepers and the nannies. I imagined how they had stared and then drawn back, averted their eyes and then looked again covertly. Had he been aware of them?

At first he had just been running round and round in a circle, and then dodging in and out of the trees, stopping every now and again to cower behind one of them, as though, they said, he were trying to get inside it. I knew, I knew. He had been shouting and singing, they thought he was drunk and then he had begun to sob. He had lain down in the long grass and rolled over and over, kicking his legs in the air, shrieking. Had they called their children away then, and hurried home, leaving him to himself? Who had telephoned for the police? Had so many people walked quickly past him? Would I not have done the same?

After a while he had taken off his shoes and socks and gone up and down the path which leads to the Round Pond, holding them up in the air and stopping in the way of anyone who came towards him, raising his fist and trying to force them to take the footwear. They had dodged him and walked on and he had pursued them and begun to snatch at their clothing. He had started to shout again. And then finally, shaking his head all the time from side to side, he had stood at the edge of the pond and slowly taken off all his clothes and piled them neatly at his feet, and when he was naked, he had waded into the water.

When he reached the centre he stood there and began to pray very loudly and then to weep and rail against God and the Devil and all the people in the park, he had threatened to drown himself in front of them. When the police came it had taken a long time for them to overpower him. They had at first tried to talk, coax, persuade him out of the water. They had sent for a doctor.

I imagined him there, ringed about by uniformed men, those people he so much dreaded, I heard their voices, impersonal, wheedling, and yet authoritative, as though they were speaking to a child. There would be the other people too, although the police would have tried to keep them back and the mothers and children would all have gone. But faces would watch him, leering, curious, between the trees, they would have whispered, taunted and accused him and perhaps found it a comic sight, too, that tall, thin, white figure growing up out of the water.

Why had I stopped looking at him as closely as I used to every day, no matter how well he seemed to be? For surely there must have been some sign that morning, something distracted or restless about him, surely I should have *known*. I might have saved him from so much.

But I see now that it was inevitable, that I could not have gone on for the rest of our lives without such an interruption, without the secret coming out. I blamed myself bitterly that day. I do not blame myself so much now.

I thought of his work, wondered how much of the poem he had completed and how long this break from it was going to be.

I was not allowed to visit him until the following morning.

I walked about the house that night as though the news had been that he was dead, I touched things which belonged to him, my head swimming. I went up into his room and stared at the table on which the piles of paper were laid out so neatly. The waste-paper basket was overflowing. I took out some of the screwed-up sheets and smoothed them over. They contained a word, or ten words, sometimes arranged in a line one beneath the other, sometimes formed into lines or half lines. Often they did not make real sense to me, they were broken and discarded bits of the jigsaw. But there was nothing to indicate any derangement in his mind over the past few days, the writing was neat and precise and orderly. I did not attempt to read what was actually on his desk. He would show it to me when he chose and until then it was no business of mine.

Half a dozen books were lying open or with markers between the pages, next to the manuscript. He had been reading Sir John Davies's *Orchestra*, and Meister Eckhardt, Kepler again, and *Utopia* and Coleridge's Notebooks. They were all so familiar to him, so thoroughly assimilated, he must only have had to check an exact wording or to re-read a passage to make certain he had completely grasped what was behind it. And yet now I read the poem I see that all these other writers lie deep below the surface and no one would discover them, the poetry and the philosophy are all his own.

I went to bed and did not sleep. I got up and made a drink and sat looking out on to the garden, dreading the next day and the state in which I would find Francis, fearing what they would do to him, wondering how he felt, lying in a strange bed in an asylum, whether he was blaming or cursing me.

Earlier, his father had telephoned me. I had scarcely been able to speak to him.

'I knew it would come to this. He has brought shame upon himself now by his own procrastination and foolhardiness. I told him something should have been done years ago. Well, he is in the best place, we may comfort ourselves with that, he will be properly looked after, properly treated.'

But do you *care*, I thought, and do you want to see him, do you . . . ?

I listened. I said nothing.

'He hasn't been up here to see us you know, not for months and months. We mean nothing to him now, he's never made any effort to understand us. He lives his life among strangers.'

And it was true, he was right to sound as he did, injured, aggrieved, complaining. But I could feel nothing for him, give him no comfort. I look back and know that I was wrong, that he was asking for help from me that night, behind the mask of self-righteousness and pride. I am older now than he was then and I understand. But at the time, I could not have understood, I could not help doing wrong.

*

I went to Battersea. It was a glorious, limpid May morning, the river danced in the sun. When I knew that I was in the street next to that leading to the hospital, I turned back and retraced my steps a hundred yards or more and then leaned against the high brick wall.

The truth was that I was not only afraid of seeing Francis, I was afraid of the other people I might come face to face with, of what forms of madness I should see, I was afraid of being shocked and distressed, and worse than that, embarrassed. I felt the flesh prickle at the back of my neck as I forced myself to go on again and turn the corner to where I saw it, that many-chimneyed red-brick prison, with the flower beds running alongside gravel paths full of tulips, very straight and waxen, heavy heads upon thin stems. As I walked across the stretch of asphalt in front of the main entrance block, a man came towards me and, at that moment, I would have turned and run back, because I was terrified, I feared that he might be a madman. He passed. I think he may have been a doctor. He looked ordinary. It was hard to tell.

So that was how the world looked at Francis now and I was one of them, I had felt that superstitious fear, I shrank from seeing and knowing, from being forced to look into that swirling, claustrophobic pit of madness.

He was with a doctor somewhere they said, I was put into a day room to wait. We had walked down long corridors. I had glimpses into wards packed tight with rows of beds like dates in a box. The place had a smell about it, I felt, as I had felt in Venice, that I could not easily breathe. I told myself that asylums were hospitals now, lunatics were patients, they were treated with understanding, given some freedom and dignity. And yet it was still terrible there and could never be anything else. It is the truth as I felt it which I have to tell.

I waited in the dayroom, which had small windows, very high up, and linoleum on the floor and tables, large, shiny tables, and upright chairs. A big room. A green, shabby, polished room. Three people in the room. A man sitting at the table playing some sort of patience, a young man with plump soft hands and a hairless baby face. He bent over the cards, moving them constantly, turning up one and then another, and laying them down again in some other place, so that in the end I realized there was no game at all, no logic behind the shifting of the cards. Perhaps it was just the sound which pleased him as they went flip-flip down on to the polished surface.

In a corner, hiding perhaps, an old woman without teeth. She looked no more than neglected, dishevelled and lonely. But no, she also looked mad, in a blank, self-absorbed way I recognized. Catching her eye, one caught only one's own reflection, there was no way of knowing her and no sign of recognition. She sat. She did not move.

And next to me, another young man, wearing a raincoat, and so perhaps another visitor. Except that he too was silent, preoccupied, I moved a little away from him, not knowing, only fearing.

There was no view out of the window, nothing to read, no pictures upon the green walls. We sat. Only the old woman was still within herself, she had learned the secret of endless, monotonous patience. Unlike the boy at the table who turned the cards over and over as the sea turns the pebbles.

We sat.

I saw not Francis but a doctor. I sat on the other side of a desk and answered questions, courteous, formal, intimate questions and, outside the window, the sun shone on stiff tulips, everything was orderly, the railings were neatly spaced around the perimeter of the building.

There was nothing I could do except tell him, everything I knew, everything that had ever happened, and it took a good deal of time, hours perhaps, the doctor wrote and wrote on sheets of foolscap paper and every mark he made was another betrayal of Francis. Yet they had to know and I have nothing to complain of, they were acting in his best interests, they treated him as well as they knew how, wanting to see him recover.

The questions went on. But there were no comments. The doctor was faintly oriental-looking, he had gingery hairs growing in tufts out of his nostrils and hairy hands like a mole's paws. He asked me about the war, always, back again and again to the war.

'It was not the war, don't you see? I realize that every other man you have in here is probably suffering as a result of the war but that is not so in Francis's case, he was well during the war, it shocked him but it did not make him mad.'

He made no comment.

'What will you do to him, what will you do? Let me take him home, now, at once, it's the only possible chance for him, don't you see, I am the only person he trusts, the only one who can be of any use, you cannot help him, you will be doing him more harm than good in here.'

But I said nothing, for how could I be sure that it was true? Perhaps I had damaged Francis beyond all hope by keeping him hidden away and struggling through the crises alone. They would not tell me. Only keep him in this place for the rest of his life, only write down judgements on their sheets of foolscap paper.

Then I tried to imagine my own future without Francis. Or rather, with daily visits of a limited duration to Francis in this hospital of stilted conversations in the day room, overheard by others and watched by the old woman.

And what would he do when I was not here? Would they let him work? But no, he would never be able to work and so he would ... what? Wander about the grounds, up and down the straight gravel paths and play games of patience and be taught to make raffia baskets and dance the Military Two-step on Saturday evening, shuffling around the gymnasium floor in the arms of some mad woman.

How would they try and treat him? By making him talk about himself? But then how would they separate his real, working, poetic voice, from the mad one, and would he even answer them, knowing that they would never understand? I dreaded other things, too, shock machines and padded cells and injections to make him hopelessly confused. I dreaded most of all that he would give up hope and relapse permanently into madness because he could no longer fight them.

I knew everything and nothing. My head was swarming with terrors and decisions and judgements and questions. I was still talking, explaining, describing, quoting this or that phrase which he used.

'It's all wrong, I tell you, it's all wrong.'

I saw the words go down on to the foolscap paper.

In the end they let me go to him. There was just room for my chair between his bed and the next, in which an old man sat up and counted his fingers energetically. He had taken off his pyjama jacket and knotted it around his waist. He was very thin, his rib cage stuck out hollow like the carcase of a chicken.

Francis was half asleep, the pupils of his eyes were very dilated. He looked strange and distant, as though his attention were fixed on something a long way off in time and place. He did not speak to me at all. Perhaps he did not know me. They had shaved him, but carelessly, so that just beneath his jaw the skin was shadowed blue and there was a small cut.

I tried not to look around me as I sat there and I kept my eyes on the ground. But there were the noises which I could not help hearing, the mutterings and sudden calls, the groans or crowing laughter, and somewhere, there was sobbing too. I felt watched and yet not seen at all, not recognized. I did not want to leave Francis there. But he seemed quite unaware of his surroundings, he seemed not to *be* Francis. It had been like looking down at a dead man. The person I knew had gone away, somewhere out of reach.

That was a terrible time. Francis was in hospital for three and a half months. But half my life seemed to pass away, I travelled from youth to middle age in the course of a summer, though I was still only thirty-six.

The weather was, until July, the most consistently good for years past, day after day the sun shone, the garden was weighed down with flowers. Visiting at Battersea was in the afternoon and quite often I walked there. I would set off after an early lunch, along the embankment and across the bridge and the river as always sparkling under a clear blue sky, the boats were like painted boats. I hated to arrive there. I would often sit on a bench in Battersea gardens and watch the mud glint yellow-gold in the sun, where the tide had receded. I went down to it and walked along, my shoes sinking into the soft rippling surface. I found an old silver buckle and a piece of driftwood shaped like a clenched fist. And after I had left the hospital and it was early evening, I would walk there again and the sky would be pink and green, the sun hit the water and sent out streaks like fire. Then the mud flats would have darkened to dark green-blue like swamps before the running tide. I walked for miles until the summer darkness fell, I never wanted to go back to the house. I ate at whatever restaurant I came upon, and drank, too, morose and silent in all the pubs of Chelsea. But the alcohol would never go to my head, so that when I reached South Terrace again, I was wide awake, I sat for hours, often until morning, in my chair and then went to bed to sleep heavily and wake with a sour taste in my mouth. Those days merge into one another in my memory, there seems to be a single stretch of time. I saw no friends, spoke only to the cleaner when she came to the house. And to Francis.

Francis.

At the beginning he did not recognize me at all and he was always drugged, his movements were slow and clumsy and his speech, if he spoke at all, difficult to understand, the voice unlike his own. He would be in the day room sometimes, and he sat as the old woman had been sitting on my first visit there, his hands hanging down between his knees, eyes staring ahead at nothing, nothing, all his attention fixed on some point within himself. He did not reply to my questions. Sometimes he would look at me. Once or twice, he told me that his head hurt him.

Then, things changed a little. Once, I found him trying to make paper boats, folding a pile of sheets this way and that, always wrongly, and then he would tear them into tiny pieces and scatter them, throw them up into the air.

'Harvey, show me what to do. I must learn to do it properly.'

It was the first time he had been aware of me and he spoke laconically, as though there was nothing unusual, nothing had happened during the past weeks.

'Show me how to get it right.'

I folded a paper boat for him and then another, taking him over each step, and he watched intently, repeating what I said under his breath. I thought of his work, of what people had written about him, of the new things which had been forming into his mind.

He was delighted with the boats, he made ten or twelve and then aeroplanes and darts, he spent an hour or more on them, and I left him still folding, folding.

The following day, the paper had all gone.

'What happened to the boats?'

'I burned them.'

They were giving him fewer sedatives and he began to talk to me earnestly, lowering his voice and making me bend my head down close to him. We were always in danger of being overheard he said, somewhere in this place people would always listen. He told me about the man in the bed next to him, who sang hymns at night, and ate like a pig and had a woman visit him who was not his wife.

'Hollowood,' he said, 'that's his name, Hollowood. Don't write it down, remember it, remember what I've told you.'

There was a woman who kept shrieking out like a mynah bird and one who had tried to cut her wrists open in the middle of the ward, and Jamie, the baby-faced boy who had been here for six years, and Marie who had given birth to a dead child and wept for it constantly, and went about the corridors and day rooms, telling people its name, Edward Joseph, and asking them to pray for it.

'You must pray, Harvey, we must all pray.'

I realized that he had become bound up in the world of the hospital, that here, everyone was curious about the others, questions were asked and endless, meandering life histories told, accusations made, here, Mrs Cruddy threw a cup of tea into a nurse's face, and Mr Dexter, who had syphilis, they said, was in the surgical wing having all his teeth out, Francis knew everything about everyone. I wondered what he had told them about himself. And yet I never *saw* any contact between patients. They averted their eyes when they passed one another in the corridors, they would come and go from the day rooms and no one would look up or speak. They were both insatiably curious about one another, and completely uninterested, wrapped up, in the last resort, only in themselves. Everyone was inquisitive. Nobody cared.

One afternoon, Francis gripped me by the arm the moment I arrived, and led me outside, we walked round and round the gravel paths while he told me that only out here would we be in no danger from the listeners.

'Harvey, they keep asking me questions, every day they make me sit in front of them, they want to know all my secrets, every private thing, they want to get inside my head.'

I knew.

'Stop them. Go and tell them not to do it. Don't you see how it is? I can't tell them, there are things ... you know what it's like.'

I knew.

He went on in the same way, pleading, explaining to me how much harm they were doing to him, how he could not think because of the confusion they had put him in.

'I've got to think, Harvey, I've got to work it all out and then I shall go to them and tell them and it will all be clear, I shall know the answers and when I've answered they'll let me come home, it will be all right, you see. It's only an examination, it's a test I have to pass, that's why they send us here, to pass, and then we can go. But I can't do it yet, I can't answer them.'

I asked him what he had been doing, whether there were any books he could read here. He looked at me in bewilderment. 'Don't you understand, I've just explained it all to you. I have to study all day and all night. I have to get it all straight in my mind and then learn how to say it. I have to pass the examination. Don't you want me to come home again?'

I was as depressed that day as I had ever been in my life. There seemed to be no hope at all for Francis. I could envisage coming here for the next twenty years and yet it was not Francis I was visiting at all, there was no real contact between us. After an hour in the hospital I went out and stared about me at the world, at the buildings flushed red by the evening sun, at buses going by full of people, at an old, long-haired man playing a ukelele at the corner of Tite Street, and I could no longer tell what was real and what I imagined, when I spoke to a barman, I heard my own voice and wondered whether it sounded odd, whether I looked peculiar, whether I might not be becoming unbalanced myself.

I badly needed something to do. But I could not concentrate on the monograph, whatever I read and wrote were equally meaningless to me. I had sunk into the sort of apathy in which Francis had so often been. Nothing mattered one way or another. I hoped for nothing, cared about nothing, the visits to the hospital were threats hanging over each day, they were times which had somehow to be endured. Nothing more. I knew and did not know how to put an end to it. I could not go on in this mood.

And then my father died, and I was shaken out of myself, I was appalled, because I had scarcely written to him for months and not at all since Francis had been in hospital, though I had known that his health was failing. But I could not bring myself to go up there and see him, I had put it off, I said it was too far, or else the effort was too great. And now he was dead and I was more full of grief than I could ever have predicted and the grief was lent an edge by all the guilt I felt. I had loved my father and I felt something else, standing there over the open grave, while the sun blazed down on our bare heads and on the white and green and golden flowers. I felt entirely alone. My mother had died years before, the other mourners were cousins and friends of my father, old business colleagues, we had scarcely met. I felt that there was no one standing between myself and the void any longer. Only Francis, and where was he?

I was away for just over a week, sorting out my father's rather muddled affairs and the break, in spite of my sadness, was what I needed, it gave me things to think about, small detailed jobs to do, I had to concentrate.

On the day I went to the hospital again after my return, Francis would not speak to me. He was sitting in the day room and when I went in he turned his back at once. He was rubbing his fingers together incessantly. I tried to make him face me and he got up and walked out quickly, shaking his head. I followed him down the corridor, caught hold of his sleeve, and he brushed me off. Finally, he locked himself in one of the lavatories, and after twenty minutes, during which I spoke to him through the door and received no reply, I left, filled with all the old despair.

I had not visited him for a week but there was no help for that, my father had died and I had told him so. He would not forgive me. I half thought of trying to talk about it to one of the doctors, but what would they say, what could they possibly do? They knew nothing about us.

That night I went home and wept, for the death of my father and the loss of Francis, sitting up at the table with my head on my arms, and then stumbled to bed and wept there too and the night seemed endless.

One morning at the end of June I was writing letters, more polite refusals to invitations for Francis to lecture here and lunch there. I had tried to keep his illness and his whereabouts a secret, I told lies about his being overworked, or simply said that he was 'away'. But once or twice recently, envelopes had arrived marked 'Please forward' and that had chilled me, I feared what people knew.

The doorbell rang twice, long, impatient rings. And I knew who he was the moment I saw him, though I would not have predicted his appearance correctly, I had a picture in my mind of someone altogether different. He was very tall and extremely handsome in a drawn, ascetic way, with a long nose and finely shaped mouth. The hair was the same, growing thick and straight, but his was almost white, and the eyes, though they were free of spectacles, were uncannily familiar, large and rather surprised.

'Mr Croft,' I said.

He was carrying a small overnight bag. He said nothing at all for several seconds, only looked at me closely, scrutinizing me. There was no sign upon his face of what judgement he made but I felt his disapproval and his intention to dislike me. I knew, I knew what was in his mind.

He said, 'I came on the overnight train from Perth.'

'Please come in.'

And of course there was every right for him to be here, it was surprising that he had not come much earlier. He was Francis's father. But a stranger to Francis, I knew that, and hostile towards me. I did not want him in the house. He began, without speaking or asking my leave, to examine it as he had examined me, he walked, very straight-backed, and less awkward than Francis, all about the sitting-room, putting on his spectacles to peer at the books and pictures, the row of objects on the mantelpiece, and then walking out and up the stairs, opening doors, inspecting. I half thought he might take out a notebook and begin to make an inventory. Most of all I resented the way he entered Francis's room and began at once to turn over the papers on his desk, to read here and there, pursing his lips. I wanted to snatch them away from him, for his assumption that he had a right to look. But most of all, he did not, could never, understand.

He flicked through some more pages, then pushed the whole lot away from him and turned to me.

'Most of this is yours, I presume.'

'This is Francis's own room.'

'I meant the house.'

'It belongs to us both. And everything in it.'

'You live ...' he paused, looking at me intently, so that I was forced to shift my glance away and ashamed at the same time for having done so, 'You live a rather *irregular* life.'

'No.'

'To me.'

'It suits us.'

He walked past me out of the room, and into the bathroom, which he also inspected closely, and then down the stairs again, and I followed him weakly, trembling with anger.

He was never a man I could have liked, we had nothing, not even Francis, in common, because our relationships with him and attitudes towards him were so utterly different. But I am sorry for him, looking back now, I understand far more. For however bad things were at that time, I still lived with the hope, even the assumption, that there was a future for us, that

I was secure with Francis and that he would, at some time or other, be well again. We were still young men. For Malcolm Croft there was only a past. Whatever he had had of Francis was in that past, and now lack of sympathy, disparity of character and way of life separated them completely. And he was an old man, seventy-two, a handsome man but facing the inevitable running down, and in his case, I thought, the loneliness and self-inflicted bitterness of old age. I do not think that I should have very much to say to him today. Except that I understand. For when one is old, there is no one to turn to and say, 'Now I see it, now I know what you were talking about, and how it was for you too. Now it is the same with me.' For they are no longer there.

He had gone back into the sitting-room.

'Naturally I do not expect to stay here.'

'It's perfectly possible, there are two spare rooms.'

'I have booked into my club.'

He sat down and, after a moment, so did I, and it felt like an interview. The room was cool and rather dark but, outside, it was already a blazing hot day.

'You are greatly to blame. Something should have been done months ago, years ago and you have been with him, you have seen how things were going. Why were no arrangements made before this?'

'You expect me to have gone to a doctor behind his back?'

'In his own best interests.'

'To have betrayed him?'

He waved a hand impatiently. 'He is as wilful now as he was when a boy, he has no idea at all of what is good for him. He does not think of others.'

'I disagree.'

He gave me a cold, dismissive look. To him, I knew nothing, was nothing, I had no right to an opinion.

'He has money. We could have helped him to go into some private nursing home. I believe there is treatment to be had abroad, in the privacy of some clinic – Austria – Switzerland ... There is no history of insanity in my family. Do you think I can accept very readily the idea that my son is deranged?'

'Do you think he can accept it?'

'He is apparently becoming quite well known in certain circles, his work has been written about in the newspapers. How are we to prevent all of this becoming public knowledge also? Have you taken any steps to try and prevent it?'

'I hope I am discreet. I have tried to handle his affairs as well as I can.'

'He was violent as a child. He had an arrogant streak. And a vicious temper. I have seen him lie upon a floor and kick because he was thwarted in some trifling way.'

'I suppose all children have tempers.'

'What do you know of children?'

He leaned across and picked a small carriage clock off the mantelpiece, tipped it upside down and read the maker's name, weighed it in his hand, set it down again. I wondered if the value had been assessed and noted.

'How long is he to be confined in this asylum?'

'At the moment it's uncertain.'

'It could perfectly well be for years. He could be there for life.'

'I think that is unlikely.'

'Are you a doctor?'

'I have been with him for a year and a half. I have seen him through this time and time again. He recovers.'

'Temporarily. Partially. One day he will not recover.'

'Is that what you want to happen?' I shouted. He ignored it.

'Do they know that he has a history of violence? He tried to murder his own brother. You will not have been aware of that.'

'He told me.'

'And if he comes out of this place are you planning to be his attendant for life?'

'When he leaves hospital, he will come here of course. This is his home.'

'Apparently. At any rate he no longer thinks of our house as his home. Perhaps that is as well. His mother would not wish to see him while he is mentally ill. She has a weak heart, she could not be distressed in that way. Some things have to be kept from her.'

'He will come here.'

'We are not a poor family. Francis has an income.'

'Yes.'

'I imagine that he earns nothing. Poetry does not pay a man a wage.'

'It has made him a little more money than you might suppose. He has a reputation now, his books are quite widely sold.'

'We are not poor. There is the house and farm, there is a considerable amount of land, managed by my younger son. There are properties.'

I waited.

'Francis is not fit to run any business.'

'I doubt if he would wish to.'

'My younger son Andrew will inherit from me. He will take over the family estate. I do not mean that Francis will be unprovided for. But *there is no money in it.*'

I wanted to hit him. I only said, 'All this is a family matter. It has nothing to do with me.'

'Quite. So long as you understand.'

I leaned forward, it seemed suddenly urgent that I should be heard and understood by this insensitive man, that I should penetrate his defences. 'Do you realize quite what an important poet Francis is? A great poet. That is what others have said, it is not only my judgement, it has been stated publicly by those whose opinions count in these things. He has written one major poem and almost finished another, he is influential and respected – do you understand that he *must* have freedom and quiet to get on with his work, because that is the reason for his existence? And if he is mad, it is because one man's brain cannot contain all the emotions and ideas and visions that are filling his without sometimes weakening and breaking down. But he will be perfectly well again, he is generally well. When he is not he is in despair and when he is fit he dreads the return of his illness. What can that be like to live with? I see him every day, I can guess, but that is all. Guess. I can't get inside his head, none of us can, he is entirely alone, there is no sharing of madness. All I can do, all anyone can do is to care for him and try to protect him, try to make the rest of his life more bearable. He needs love and tolerance and patience and help and God knows all that is hard enough to give, sometimes it is impossible. I have almost left here and never come back, because I thought I could no longer cope. I dare not think ahead. I dare not assume that I shall always, somehow, manage to carry on. But I have to try. That is the only thing that seems important. To try. Because Francis relies upon me, as he has never relied upon anyone. You may not believe that or understand it, but I know it. I *know*.'

He had been watching me, his eyes had not flickered as I spoke and at that moment I almost lost my temper again and struck him to try and elicit some response, some acknowledgement. His hands were placed palm to palm in front of him, he looked like the stone effigy of a man at prayer. The fingers were long, the exact shape of Francis's fingers.

He said, 'You have your own work.'

'Yes.'

'But that is not important to you?'

'Yes. In a limited way. Francis's work is of far greater importance.'

'To him?'

'To anyone. That is a qualitative judgement.'

'I confess I find you hard to understand.'

'I'm sorry.'

'You see yourself as some kind of guardian angel.'

He was smiling, a faint, sarcastic, indulgent smile, I had seen it occasionally on Francis's own face. They were so very alike and so different.

'I do not.'

But that was untrue, I knew it as I denied it, he was mocking me for taking myself seriously, for the figure I was trying to cut in my own eyes and now, in his. He did not know anything about me and yet he had perceived something of the underlying truth of my nature.

'Well, you are a grown man. Francis is a grown man. You must live your own lives. Now I shall take a taxi to my club. Perhaps you will meet me at the hospital at two thirty?'

'Don't you prefer to see him alone?'

'No.'

I wondered if he was afraid of the place, as I had been, and still was, or if he felt that he needed me as a shield between

himself and Francis. Or else whether he wanted to see us together in order to judge even more accurately how things were.
I did not want to go there with him. I did not know how
Francis would take an unexpected visit from his father, whom
he did not love and had not seen for so long, who disapproved
of him and favoured the younger son. Can that all have been
true? That he took no interest at all in Francis? No, no, it was
not true, I have come to see now how thick Malcolm Croft's
walls of defence were and yet that something – affection, un-
certainty, disappointment, lay behind them. I could not reach
him. Perhaps no one ever did so. I think that he was one of the
most unhappy men I have ever met. Francis had once said of
him, 'He wears a mask to hide the mask lying behind it.'

When we met at the hospital that afternoon, he stood for
some minutes staring at the red-brick building. Then he said,
'The gates are open.'
    'Why not?'
    'I remember an asylum not far from the place in which I
grew up. It had spiked railings and barbed wire and a gatekeeper
with keys. But people were still afraid to pass it. I have even
seen men cross themselves. They would take the longer road to
avoid the place. There was an alarm bell which sounded if any
of the patients escaped. I remember the sound of it. People
locked their doors.' He glanced around him. There were houses
very close by. 'Is that how they feel here?'
    I shook my head. 'But things have changed perhaps. Besides,
there are degrees of illness ...'
    'Of madness, madness, why do you not say what you mean?
Am I afraid to speak out?'
    'No.'
    And then, just once, for a moment, I caught a glimpse behind
the mask. He asked anxiously, 'How shall I find him?'
    'It's hard to say. Perhaps very silent and depressed – he may
not say much to you. Perhaps excited, edgy.'
    'Raving?'
    I was not entirely sure what he meant, what pictures of
Francis were forming in his mind.
    'What he says doesn't always make sense. He becomes

obsessed with a certain idea, he repeats some phrases over and over again. But no – not raving.'

He nodded. We went on, through the gates.

No, Francis was not raving. He was quiet. He looked tired. But he looked himself, for the first time since he had come here. He was in the day room writing and when we entered he looked up and seemed quite unsurprised, he only turned the sheet of paper over quickly and laid his arm across it.

'So you've come to see the prodigal. Hello, Harvey, you didn't tell me, did you?'

'I didn't know.'

He seemed to believe me. And then, for a while, he took no further notice at all of his father.

'I'd like some chocolate, Harvey, will you bring it tomorrow, and a better shaving mirror, the ones they have here are no use. Oh, they let me shave myself now, didn't I tell you? I suppose they think I can be trusted with a razor. And I need some more paper and a notebook, one of the black bound ones. I've got a lot of things to put down. And my own fountain pen. I want some books, too. I'll make a list and you must bring them in my briefcase, the one with the lock, I need to lock everything away, people do steal so here, you can't imagine.'

Then he leaned back. 'Well, father, how are you?'

They talked for half an hour. After a while, I left them and went out to buy the chocolate. Francis was gentle, he had asked about the family and the farm, and he listened, and nodded when his father told him he had done the right thing in coming here for treatment. Though he also looked at me. 'It was Harvey,' he said. 'He arranged it in the end. He saw to everything.'

But he did not sound resentful. I decided that he had had no recollection at all of the day in the park. He went on with easy, slightly formal social conversation, there appeared to be nothing whatsoever wrong with him. I did not know how he really felt, whether he was glad to see his father, whether he would blame me afterwards for bringing him here. I felt hopeful again. Somehow or other he had come through, and perhaps that meant they would let him return home, that he would be able to continue with his work.

When I got back from the shop, Malcolm Croft was telling

him about some accident to one of the farmworkers. Francis sat, not moving, his eyes all the time resting on his father's face. I thought that he had inherited the same way of masking his thoughts, all his emotions. He did not appear to notice my return but when I put the chocolate in front of him, he ate it all, breaking it neatly into squares and setting them out in a pattern on the table, and when he had selected a piece, he re-arranged the others.

Someone came into the room, an elderly, balding man with a glass eye, and noticing him, Francis jumped up and went and took him by the arm, and brought him over to us.

He said, 'This is Victor and you must both be very very good to him because he's a friend, he's my only friend in this place.'

Victor's face was expressionless. He bit his lip. We each of us shook hands with him on Francis's insistence, and were too embarrassed to meet one another's eyes.

'We talk together, Victor and I, and he explains the ways of the world to me, he tells me all about the things I don't know. I've led such a limited life, I need to be told everything I don't understand. He was a clown in a circus, he *knows*. We go for walks and there isn't anything we don't tell each other. He's the only friend I've got.'

Victor's skin was dead-looking, he was emaciated, and life-less. I had not seen him here before. I suspected in fact that he and Francis knew nothing about one another.

'I sail,' Victor said then, 'I go sailing a good deal now, I asked how to make the wheels go round, I worked it out for myself with charts, and now they've given me my own boat, I take cargo mainly. Peacocks have good tails, there's a profit to be made there if you know how, and comets too.'

Malcolm Croft stood up. He had seen only a little and he could not take it. I was used by now to the Victors of this place, and to the way Francis swung about, appearing to be quite sane, to know what he was saying, and then speaking some involved nonsense. We left. Victor had gone to sit in an armchair right at the other side of the room and Francis did not come with us, he turned his back and picked up a sheet of paper on which he had been writing.

Outside, the midsummer heat rose like steam from the

asphalt. The lawns were yellowed and patchy. I remembered our time in Dorset the previous year, thought of how the gorse would smell on the barrow. I wondered if we would go there before this summer was over. Malcolm Croft walked in silence beside me. At the river we stopped and stood looking down at the water, the sun full on our backs.

I said, 'You see how things are.'

'But at least he's in control of himself. I expected ...'

'Oh yes.'

'He knew who I was.'

I remembered the days when I had gone there and been unrecognized.

'Perhaps there is something to be said for that.'

'I think he is in fact much better.'

He turned to me. 'But not *well*. Not well. He is not a normal man, is he? Not clear in his mind, not in full command of his faculties.'

'But still better than he was,' I insisted. 'If you had seen ...'

'You have no idea what I have seen. And you have no idea what it is like to visit your own son in a lunatic asylum.'

For a short while, I had again thought that we n.ight find some bond between us, sufficient to make at least for a mutual tolerance. I had been wrong. I asked if he would come back to South Terrace and have some tea, because I felt guilty, I should have been kinder towards him. He frowned. 'Have you thoughts about the future? When you and he are old men? Does that never enter your mind?' His voice was thick with resentment.

'Yes.'

'It is all very puzzling to me.'

'Not really. I hope you'll come and see him again.'

'Do you? Does he? And what shall I find?'

I shrugged and tried to imagine this man at Francis's age, with young children, a future, hopes. Very many men of seventy had lost their sons in the war. He might have comforted himself that both of his were still alive. I said as much now.

'Is that what you believe?'

'Of course.'

'Then you are wrong. I had rather he were dead than this, there would have at least been no shame in it, I should not have had to wake every morning of my life and fear for his future. At least I should have known. At least I should not have that.'

I saw then how much he loved Francis, how much he had planned for him and how disappointed he was now, how bitter and shocked to have seen him in the hospital. I believed what he told me, that, to him, Francis would have been better dead and buried in Flanders.

Then, there was no hope at all of sympathy left between us.

He hailed a taxi and shook hands with me, unsmiling, unbending. I watched him drive away, saw the back of his head which was so much the same shape as Francis's. If it had been possible, I would have returned to the hospital at once, for I badly needed to find out what Francis thought, whether he had been upset or angered by his father's visit.

In fact, I was never to know. The following day, I simply told him that Malcolm Croft had spent the night at his club and gone back to Scotland by the morning train, that I had not seen him again. Francis nodded, and waved his hand dismissively. He said, 'Harvey, I've got to work, I've got to get out of here. I'm perfectly all right, I don't understand why they've brought me, but it's all over and done with. I must get out. You must tell them.' He was not speaking with the old, intense, crazed voice, he was quiet, firm, clear-headed. I knew that, for the moment, it was true, things were better.

He spoke very little at first, that day I went to fetch him. I had kept a taxi waiting, but he preferred to walk, there was so much he wanted to look at. He peered into front windows of the houses, whose lawns were baked hard by the past few weeks of sun. There were few flowers here. Dogs ran about, mangy, mongrel dogs, very thin. As we walked alongside the last of the warehouses, Francis said, 'It's like that street in Oxford.' I had been reminded of it every day, there was the same run-down look about all these streets, the houses were closed in upon one another.

Francis had not glanced back at the hospital. We had gone around his ward, he had shaken hands with a dozen or more patients and they had stared at him dully, perhaps not registering that he was leaving, probably not caring.

Half way across Battersea Bridge we stopped to watch a cargo boat sail slowly out from underneath us and away in the direction of the open sea. Francis shook his head. 'It feels ...' He did not go on. The water folded over and over on either side of the moving ship and the waves extended right to the edges of the river, the houseboats rocked a little on their moorings. It was close and thundery, the sky sullen, hazy yellow.

'Harvey, I don't want to know what happened. Why you sent me there. I don't remember and I don't want to know. It doesn't matter now.'

'I didn't send you. I knew nothing about it.' That I had to say. But he shook his head again fiercely, raised his voice at me. 'I don't want to *hear*.'

'I'm sorry.'

'You see, they don't believe me. They said I was better, that they were letting me go home and I told them that I always get better in the end, it is always all right eventually, I only had to wait. I could have waited at home, I needn't have taken up their time. But they didn't listen to me. And all the others staying there – they won't get better – they've nothing to live for. Harvey, how can they sit there and know that? Why don't they do away with themselves? I would. Oh, don't look so bothered, I'm *all right*.'

'Yes.'

'It's awfully hot.'

'The garden's past its best. The roses are over, everything's been so dry. I'm sorry there's nothing much left for you to see.'

'It doesn't matter. If I start to tell you what happened, about the days in there, how they went on and on and on, and sometimes I thought I should slit my wrists just because I was so bored and the nights never came to an end either, and I was terrified of never being home again ... listen ... you must not let me tell you.'

'If you want to talk about it.'

'No.'

'Why not?'

'Because it's all done with.' And he caught hold of me and spun me round and round in a sort of wild dance, laughing, shouting with relief and delight. 'Oh God, you don't know how I feel, you cannot imagine how I feel.'

'Perhaps I can.'

'Yes.' He took my arm and we walked slowly on, over the bridge and up through Chelsea.

'I'd like a boat. Could we go somewhere on a boat?'

'Of course. Whatever you like.'

'No. I couldn't work. Do you know I can remember exactly where I got to in the poem, the last line I wrote is in my head. There's such a muddle in between as though I've been asleep … but I remember that absolutely. Now I've got to get on. There isn't much left to do.'

'Don't tire yourself.'

'No. How do I look?'

His eyes were bright, he looked elated and yet puzzled, too, as though he were uncertain of his surroundings, and was holding on to my arm for support.

I smiled, 'Really pretty well.'

'I feel dizzy.'

'Perhaps it's the sun.'

'No. It happens on and off. Don't worry about it.'

When we turned the corner into South Terrace, he stopped dead. He said, 'It's the same.'

'Of course. You haven't been away so long really.'

'It feels like a hundred years. I'm not the same person. I expected – the houses haven't changed. But they don't look real to me. I don't feel as if I'm here. I can't be.'

'You are.'

'Shall I be all right now?'

'Yes.' It was true. He would be well for a time, perhaps for as long as before, two years, in which there was so much work he would do. Perhaps it would be longer, the stay in hospital might have done him some lasting good, the madness might never come back to him. But they had not said so. They had been cautious, unwilling to make any predictions. I must watch, they said, always watch. I felt like a jailor.

Francis put out his hand and ran it over the surface of the front door like a blind man, his face suffused with a sort of amazement. When we got inside, he went all around the house in the same way, touching, gazing, not speaking. But when he reached his own room, he looked at the desk and turned abruptly away, brushing a hand over his forehead.

He went to bed and slept until late in the evening, when the thunder had just begun to rumble around, the sky was closing in, dark as a bruise over the river. Great spats of rain were falling on to the garden steps, big as beans. Francis stood at the window, watching them, waiting for the storm.

A week later, we went to Kerneham, and there he finished 'Earth, Air, Water, Fire', working for so many hours a day that I thought he must surely make himself ill again. But he seemed to thrive on it, it was such a relief to him to be writing again, the ideas, he said, filled up his head and overflowed as fast as he could get them down. He often got up in the middle of the night, I would hear a noise and always woke at once, I so much dreaded incidents like those of the previous year. When I found him, he would be reading aloud through what he had written during the day, sometimes repeating a couple of lines over and over again, and then altering a word or the order of words. The first three sections of the poem had gone slowly. The last he reeled through, but then he re-wrote it five or six times. When he went out, walking, he muttered aloud to himself. But he looked rested, he ate enormous meals and slept well. He said he had not felt better or more happy for years.

Just before the poem was finished, he wanted a break, and so we went walking for three days, over the downs as far as Swanage. It was the loneliest of journeys, we saw almost no one. Only sheep, and birds flying high over the barrows, kites and larks and a peregrine. It was dull weather, gusty, rather cold, for much of the time the tracks were muddy and a mist hung over the countryside, we could never see more than half a mile ahead of us. It did not seem to matter, it was even something of a relief, for I had come to associate hot summer weather with Francis's madness. I think he felt the same. He said that he could breathe now. He wrote one or two poems at that time, in a small notebook he always carried, when we had found somewhere to stay for the night. The beautiful 'Child's dance' and the three 'Bee Poems' came then, and they seemed to have been formed in a quite separate part of his mind from the long poem, it is hard to find anything which places them in the same period.

When we got back to Kerneham, two letters had come. One for me: an invitation to write a long, comprehensive book on the whole Egyptian civilization – it was to be both popular and scholarly. At first, I simply tossed the letter aside. It seemed out of the question. I was a worker in miniature, I took minute fragments of my subject and analysed them in detail. But Francis told me I should change my mind, to him the project was a marvellous idea, it was something for me to 'get my teeth into', something different and ambitious.

'You must, Harvey, don't you see why? You must have something of your own and something large, that will take up all your energy and time. This is ideal. You've no idea how much good it will do you to have something long to write. It worries me, you see, having you devote yourself exclusively to me. It makes me feel uncomfortable. Besides, my dear, think of the money, think of the money.'

But there was another letter. To Francis from an American University, asking him to deliver their annual oration, and to be resident with them for eight weeks. In addition, he was to receive the Schoenbaum Gold Medal, which had never, I knew, been bestowed upon anyone nearly so young. I took it for granted that he would refuse, not the medal, but the invitation to lecture and stay in California. He said nothing at all about it for a day. Instead, he finished the poem and went for a walk on the barrow.

When he returned, I was in the kitchen. He stood in the doorway.

'Harvey . . .'

I glanced at him and away again, afraid.

'Two things. One, you are going to write this Egyptian book. You must. And I shall go to California.'

He came across the small room. His face was determined and also full of concern.

'It will be,' he said, 'the very best thing, at the moment. For me. And for you. You may not think that that is true. It is. I *have* to try and stand on my own two feet again.'

'You'll go for the full two months?'

'Yes.'

'And when you come back?'

'Why, everything will be just the same. Of *course*.'

He put his hands on my shoulders. 'Harvey, you must not worry about me. You must not.'

That was impossible. I thought that if the doctors knew of his plan to go to California, they would unquestionably veto it, unless I were to accompany him. But for Francis, that would not do, he could not put only half a foot forward. And I saw why. I saw that he must go, and by himself.

I told him so, and then went on preparing our supper. We opened a bottle of hock to celebrate the completion of the poem. Nothing more was said about the new plan that night.

But on September 3, he sailed for California.

*

Harvey,

This is the most marvellous place in the world, you cannot imagine how marvellous it is. Think that they might never have asked me, and then, oh, what I should have missed. It is like some kind of paradise. To begin with the people are the nicest, most generous, interested, sympathetic and kind, they give me all I could ever want and more. I have the whole floor of a house to myself, with a huge study overlooking the woods and they don't disturb me at all. Which is an irony because I am not working, I have nothing whatsoever in my head, no ideas, and I don't intend to conjure up any. For the time being I must take it in and look around me all over again, and there are things here I have never seen the like of! I read and I watch the woods. You will never have seen trees like these, they are the most amazing colours, poinsettia red and olive and copper.

I am reading American authors, which is as it should be: Whitman and Hawthorne, but Melville most of all, Melville is the finest American writer, I cannot take him in, I shall have to go back to the beginning again. But they will explain him to me here, they are very learned and patient, or else if they do not, the country itself will somehow do so. If I could write something that contained so much meaning as *Moby Dick* ... Well, that's what I plan to do one day, a huge allegory. There's room to think in those terms here. I have been writing cramped, tight poems on that little island of yours. Now I want to begin something which will take me at least five years. But there is nothing to put into it yet.

I have been away with a friend. I have a million friends here but chiefly one called Don Kirst, who is a junior Professor, and a year older than me. He looks like a totem pole. I mean his face is that dark reddish colour of wood and his features are somehow flattened, he might have been carved out of a totem pole.

He has been taking me all over the place, I have seen the seven wonders of the world, they are all here in this state. We saw the fruit farms in the Santa Clara valley: it is like Spain or Greece here, it is always, always hot and the skies are not blue they are almost white and the sun looks altogether larger, and there are long, hard shadows. They have peach farms. Think!

We went to Emerald Bay, which *is* emerald, I have never seen water like it, absolutely still and clear and green, shining like a great jewel. We went into the mountains, then, in among the redwood trees. But California is really no good for writers, this is a painter's country. It dazzles me. I wake up every morning and cannot believe in all this colour, one's eyes are not up to it. I realize that we spend most of our time in England living among browns and duns and all that fog. But I hope that somehow what I see here is sinking in through the pores of my skin.

We came back yesterday. Don knows the whole state as well as you know Kerneham, he lived here as a boy, he went hunting and fishing, and lived outside for weeks at a time on his own. And now he is a Professor of English specializing in the eighteenth century, so urbane and good-mannered! Americans have the most superb manners. He is very funny but he doesn't laugh much himself, so I laugh for him. He has promised to take me up into the Rockies for a few days. We shall camp out. I want to stay here forever.

I have to talk to the undergraduates, and they are so enormously respectful, it frightens me. They take down every little thing I say and that is a situation I am so unnerved by, that I end up just reading poetry to them, and then I lie awake at night making up wise and poetic and witty phrases with which to bemuse them, and then I have forgotten them all by morning!

I am entertained all the time to marvellous meals, and I drink too much because California wine is remarkably good. Everything here is good. I have written not one jot nor one title. There are much more important things. I'm so well. It was all I needed. I shall never be ill again now, I have got the measure of myself. They know nothing of all that here. Why should they?

Well, next week we go off like Huck Finns and I shan't be able to tell you anything about it until we return because we shall be quite out of touch with the world of writing paper and mail boxes. Don says I shall have to grow a beard. I'm not certain if I shall like that but it would be something else to hide behind.

*

He went on his expedition. He wrote pages to me about it. It was like nothing he had ever dreamed of. He would, he told me, be most likely to stay for longer than originally planned.

I read his letters through very quickly and in utter misery and then burned them, as he had always burned things he loathed. I scrubbed the ashes into a powder. I would have left them unopened and unread if I had had the strength of mind. There was never anything but this wild, ecstatic joy in everything he saw and in everyone he met. I was hurt and resentful, and afraid, too, knowing as I did where this sort of intense excitement led and what followed. Well then, let it follow, and let his new friend care for him, nurse him through the fits of despair and hold him back when he tried to beat his head against the walls, let him lie awake every night, alert for the faintest sound, let him ...

I was ashamed of my own bitterness and powerless to contain it. I wrote short, stiff letters of reply to Francis, and in the end, I did not reply at all. He did not seem to notice and every few days I would receive six or seven pages of enthusiastic narrative. He made no references to London or to the recent past, it might never have existed, it was as though he had cut all his ties. Once only he referred to my book.

I was writing and loathing it, every day I had to drag myself to my desk, or to the British Museum reading room. It was partly that a long, dense but relatively straightforward book of this sort seemed to me, at that time, a waste of my time and scholarship. I do not now think this was so. I was a very arrogant young man. Looking at the few books I have produced in my lifetime, I see that it is by far the best, if only because it reached the widest audience, it taught more about the beauties and truths of the Egyptian civilization than anything else I had ever done, in my limited, esoteric way. But I could not have been writing it at a worse time. I was lonely. I missed and was deeply envious of Francis and I worried about him constantly, I hated and resented his new friendship. For the past three years our lives had been apparently inextricably bound up together, he had relied utterly upon me. Now he had broken clean away. I had not expected him to manage it so successfully. Perhaps I did not want him to. I had been prepared, at the beginning, for the cry for help. None had come. Oh, on the contrary!

For the few friends I saw during that time I must have been sour company. I had no interest in anything outside myself and my own misery. I went to a few concerts and the music irritated me. I took to reading detective stories, some times two a day, and went through them blindly, forgetting everything about them the moment I closed the cover. London was foggy for most of that autumn, we groped about clinging to walls and railings, and my lungs and mouth seemed to be always thick with the damp.

A year ago we had been in Venice and I had thought I could never be more miserable and depressed in any city than I had been there. But London was worse.

Francis should have been home for Christmas.

*

Harvey,

I think I shall stay here at least until February. Though at last winter has come, the trees are all bare. But their trunks are still the most marvellous colours, all shades of brown and grey, and the light streams between them, it is always so clear here, everything is so bright, so much more substantial, everything *vibrates*. But it is colder.

I am going to the coast for Christmas, near Monterey, where Don's family live. But they will be away in Boston, and we shall have the house to ourselves. It is on rocks, almost *in* the sea, with beautiful cliffs and trees behind. I have seen pictures of it.

The best way to travel in this country is by rail, you cannot think how beautiful some of those journeys are. I have a desire now to go all over America on a slow train. It would take two or three years and that would not matter, it might be the best thing I could do with my life.

I have been presented with my medal. You may have read about all the song and dance there was. I felt rather drunk and very vain. Now I'm reading Poe, which is dark and clever.

My official time here is over of course, but I may stay on unofficially. I have still nothing to write. The proofs of the poem have come but I can't go through them yet, my head is so full of other things.

*

The more often he wrote to me, the farther away he seemed to grow. I believed, at this time, that he would never come back. Christmas passed. I worked the whole time on my book, locked away in my study at South Terrace, and at night, went out to walk the streets, looking up into other people's lighted windows, seeing their Christmas trees. I was eaten up with bitterness. No man should allow himself to sink so low.

And then in the middle of January, after a break of eleven days, another letter came.

Harvey,

Last night I had to get up and go outside, I couldn't breathe and then I heard the wolves baying and the eagles fly by night here, their eyes gleam, they circle and circle overhead so I knew that they had found me. We saw vultures too, hanging very still in the dead sky. But it is only what I expected because people do not forget and when my brother shot the bird, I had to try and kill him. I am waiting to be punished, the message will come now, it is the only way and the light is so strong, there is never anything now but this light, night does not seem to come at all here, you can see all the way through the sky and into the face of the sun. It burns my eyes, I have to draw the curtains, but they are thin, and fortunately I have a cottage near by with a roof of straw and I was able to find a torch and set it alight and it burned well. So you will understand the saying about the men who are sent to sea. I mean, taken by the press gang and it is the truth, here I have seen women walking about in terrible fear and anyone may take me away, so you will never see me. They have got together and collected money and written a letter about me, and so I have learned to swim, which is my only hope but I fear the animals now and all the stars have sharpened points. Please tell me, please leave it and they will take only days to reach you and if you are not there, use the telescope. PLEASE.

Towards the bottom of the paper the writing had become smaller, more and more difficult to read, the letters slid into one another. It lay on my desk. I stared at it and had no idea what to do, whether to leave at once, or wait here, whether to write or to telegraph his friends in America, explaining to them. His letter had taken a fortnight to arrive. He might already be in a hospital somewhere.

The following day, I received a cable. 'Francis sailed for England Thursday. Kirst.'

He never posted to me the letters he wrote on board ship. I did not find them until after his death, among his papers, and only then could I understand what an appalling journey he had had, and how alone he had been, for by the time he arrived, he could not speak about it, he was too ill.

*

Harvey,
If I lock my door I can pretend the sea is no longer there. I went out on to the deck this morning and I almost jumped over the rail. I had to hold on to it. The sea goes on and on, it spreads like blood and there is a small circle of it flat and grey painted

157

upon the wall of my cabin and sometimes a gull flies across. Nothing else.

But yesterday they buried one of the passengers and perhaps that is only the beginning. A man had a heart attack and we were not supposed to know, but the word spread around like mist, brushing against everyone in turn and in the early morning they buried him. I got up. I watched them. The body was sewn into a canvas bag and they tipped it very gently into the water. I was grateful to them for that. There was scarcely a splash. Then what? For here are no burrowing worms and no flames to consume, only a slow, seeping damp, the flesh swells and bursts open like a plum in the water and those are the pearls that were his eyes. And it was beautiful, the sailors grouped at sunrise around the body.

If I lock my door. But the engines throb through my head, the whole body of the ship judders and shakes like a demented man, I cannot stop it, they will do nothing about it for me, and there is only the sea beyond the door, no houses or streets, no friendliness.

Yesterday I wrote a poem about my father. Something is going to happen to us out here, and I shall never reach home, I shall be sent backwards and forwards across this grey water for ever and that will be my punishment. And there was the blinding light, I thought that it would never end. I find now that I am very guilty, I read of it yesterday.

'Think of your many years of procrastination, how the gods have repeatedly granted you further periods of grace of which you have taken no advantage. It is time now to realize the nature of the universe to which you belong and of that controlling power whose offspring you are. And to understand that your time has a limit to it. Use it then to advance your enlightenment or it will be gone and never in your power again.'

So I have sat at the table here for four hours trying to work, because of all those weeks I squandered, time when I have been eating and drinking and listening to concerts, and wandering about in all that brightness and I have contributed nothing at all, I have not justified my existence and the breath I have taken in and the bread I have eaten. But I cannot, cannot write, I have nothing to say. There is only the throbbing inside and outside my head and the sea turns over and over and leaves no mark. I should be sewn into a sack and toppled into the water and then at least I should be food for the Leviathan.

I do not go into the dining-room now, I am fasting, and also, the knives and forks clash and catch against the light and flash a pain through my eyes, and all the mouths of the people are opening and shutting. I will put my head into the mouth of the great whale. But at night the stars come out, there are the planets Jupiter and Saturn and Mars and then I can pray and in the very early morning, there are angels dancing on the face of the waters.

I am very tired. You promised never to send me away and twice you have sent me away. It smells of oil inside this ship and the doors hiss as they close and wherever I go, someone watches me, I hear a faint footstep and look quickly around but they are always just vanishing out of sight, their laughter is all that is left ringing on the air. And so I walk mostly at night, it is quiet then and the sea is dark, at night there is no danger.

> The many men so beautiful
> And they all dead did lie,
> And a thousand, thousand slimy things
> Lived on, and so did I.

*

There are also two notebooks which he filled during that journey but most of the entries make little sense, they are long lists of words about the dazzling light or the noise of the ship's engines. But there are one or two fragments, as though he had been desperately trying to write a poem about the things he had seen in California. Some of the lines are about vultures and he also mentions a marvellous waterfall which lay at the heart of a forest. One is about the waves which came pounding over the rocks towards the house at Monterey, until they seemed to take on the shape of wolves with slavering tongues and foaming mouths, reaching out to devour him.

As far as I could tell this burst of madness had struck him all at once, it had not, as before, crept up on him gradually, leaving a few more traces day by day. He had been gloriously happy, everything he saw and did was glowing with life and beauty, and then a black hood was dropped over him, and he was suffocating, the nightmares danced inside his head, he was trapped. He fled for home.

I was shocked when I saw Francis, perhaps because, after a separation of three months, I had forgotten how ill he could look. I went on board the ship at Southampton and found his cabin. He was sitting on the bed. Half his belongings were packed haphazardly into an open suitcase and a holdall, the rest were strewn about the floor and a table – books, clothes, manuscripts, photographs, all muddled together.

His skin was sallow from a fading suntan and there were dark circles below his eyes, which were dull and staring. His hair had grown quite long and it splayed out over his collar and fell forward into his eyes. I stood in the doorway for a few seconds, looking at him, trying to understand what I felt. It was mainly relief that he was back and that nothing had happened to him on the voyage. I felt a rush of the familiar concern and of misery that he was no better and never would be, that after all, there had been no cure. But more than anything else I felt myself re-orientated. Francis was back. I had not only been unhappy, but I had felt my life to be entirely lacking in purpose, while he had been away. Caring for him had not merely taken up most of my time during the past two years : it had changed me as a person. I was no longer answerable to and for myself alone, nor did I wish to be. When I acted it was for us both. I had become used to that, I had grown into my role. The last weeks had shaken me, because they seemed to have stripped me of any significant reason for my existence. I had work to do about which I did not particularly care. That was all. Now, standing in that cluttered, stifling cabin, I felt a complete person again, I saw that I needed to have someone entirely dependent upon me, and it surprised me, because I had always assumed that I was solitary by nature.

'Francis ...'
He jumped in alarm. 'Who is it?'
I went closer to him.
'Harvey?'

'Of course.'

'I'm sorry. I seem to have put my spectacles down ... or dropped them ... someone's taken them ... I don't remember. It doesn't matter. There was nothing I wanted to see.'

'We'll find them. I'd better help you pack.'

'Where are we?'

'Southampton. Home.'

'Oh yes. Yes, of course.'

'I've brought a car down. I thought you might not want to face the train – all that standing about on platforms and so forth. It's snowing.'

'Yes.'

I turned to one of the suitcases and began to sort out his shirts and socks, I had my back to him. The next moment he had hurled himself at me, I was sent flying face forwards over the table, his full weight was on top of me, and he had his hands tightly around my neck. It took me only a moment to regain my balance and force him away. I was far stronger than he was – he looked as if he had eaten very little for weeks. His only advantage over me had been that of surprise. I got his hands away from my neck and pushed him into the chair, keeping hold of him by the shoulders. He had collapsed forwards, there was no strength or resistance left in him. He was shivering violently. I had no idea why he had attacked me, and I had to try and put it out of my mind, because somehow I must finish his packing, get him off the ship and home without anyone knowing what had happened. I had no idea what he might try to do next, or if I could control him. But he leaned back and closed his eyes, his face was blenched white beneath the tan.

I said, 'It's all right. We're going home.'

'I don't believe you. You're taking me somewhere, aren't you?'

'No. I'm taking you home.'

He leaned forward again, half rising to his feet, he began to shout. 'Where are you going to take me? Oh, I know, I can't trust any of you, I can't believe you any longer, you've been talking to them here, you'll put me in a sack and drop me into the water, you'll send me into hospital again.'

'*No*, Francis.' I gripped his wrists. 'I'm taking you home. I swear I am taking you home. There will be nobody else there.'

He dropped his hand on to his chest. I thought that he was crying but he seemed only to be struggling for breath. I had finished packing his things, shoving them all anyhow into the cases. In the corridors outside, there were voices, footsteps, the noise of luggage trolleys and from somewhere else in the dock a liner hooted and hundreds of gulls rose screeching into the air. I handed Francis his overcoat and he fumbled, getting it on, his hands were trembling too violently to do up the buttons.

'I haven't slept, not for weeks, not since I left for America. I daren't sleep.'

'You will when we get home.'

The doctor had prescribed some sleeping tablets for me, just after Francis went away. I would not need them myself now, but I could give one to him.

In fact, he went to sleep in the car almost before we were out of Southampton, he lay across the back seat with his head on a rug and his luggage piled about him on the floor, and slept as deeply as some hibernating animal. It snowed heavily all the way, the fields on either side of the roads were high and rounded like pillows and the flakes whirled hypnotically in the path of my headlamps. I had to keep blinking to prevent myself from losing all sense of direction. We were not back in London until well after ten o'clock. When I turned off the engine there was complete silence. Francis opened his eyes but for a long time he did not move. I could see the pale bones of his face in the white reflection from the snow on the roof-tops.

Then he said, 'There hasn't been much time.'

'For what?'

'There used to be a lot of time when I was quite all right.'

'You will be again.'

'I can't do any work. I can't make things go together somehow. It's all ...' He turned his head. 'It's snowing.'

'Yes.'

'There was no snow there. Nothing so beautiful as snow. Everything was hard and bright. It hurt my eyes so.'

'We'd better go inside. It's cold.'

'What have you done to your collar?'

I put my hand up and felt that it was twisted, my tie was pulled half way around my neck. I set it straight again. Francis said, 'That's better.' He clearly did not remember his attack on me.

Yet he seemed to be better, even in this short time. He went into the house and put some of his things away, glanced at a few letters and he looked simply tired.

I was wrong. He was very ill indeed for most of that night, he kept waking and trying to get out of the house, he wept when I restrained him, and called out that they were putting him in a bag and dropping his body into the sea. In the end, I managed to get him to take two of my sleeping tablets.

Early the following morning, I telephoned to a friend for the address of a specialist he had mentioned to me in some other context while Francis was away. I made an appointment with the doctor, whose name was Meredith, but when I explained what kind of state Francis was in, he said that I should not leave him at present, but that he would come to South Terrace himself.

'That might not be a good idea. He is very much afraid of doctors – his experiences in Battersea seem to have shaken him. I've promised him I will never let him go back there. I'm very much afraid of alarming him.'

'There's no need for him to know that I'm a doctor. I can visit as an acquaintance of yours. I should only like to have a look at him and form an idea of his state. Presumably it will be possible for you to try and speak to me apart from him.'

'It should be, yes.'

'Don't worry about things.'

He sounded reassuring, he had taken in the situation at once, but I dreaded that Francis would somehow find out the truth, that I should have betrayed him yet again. What I wanted was advice, a frank opinion of how things were likely to go in the future and what I ought to do. I no longer felt able to take the decisions and face the full responsibility entirely alone. I wanted above all to know that I was doing Francis no harm.

The day Meredith came he was subdued and rather bleary-eyed. He read a little in the morning, but then fell asleep again and he was still in bed when the doorbell rang, so that everything I had to say could be said.

It was snowing again outside, I watched it fall as I talked, and I remembered the afternoon Francis and I had been together in the Sussex library, and how it had been snowing then beyond the tall windows. The owl which had come like a banshee through the wood towards us on our walk that night had seemed to Francis an omen of evil, he had been terrified by it, though he had stayed silent, I had not known his feelings at the time. Perhaps he had been right.

Dr Meredith listened and I found that I was talking about myself now, about my resentment and anger and unhappiness while Francis had been in California. The room had gone dark. I felt drained and light as a cork, relieved. I went over to switch on the lamps.

I said, 'And now it is all happening again, it is as bad or worse. What is there to be done? I have to know the truth. You do see that? I cannot go on from day to day, taking risks with him any longer. But the medical profession seems to enjoy keeping its secrets. I could get nothing out of them at Battersea.'

He removed his small, wire-rimmed spectacles and began to clean them slowly. He said, 'What seems to you the best thing for him? What do you think he needs?'

'Oh, I haven't much doubt that he should be here with me, or else somewhere in the country. Wherever he chooses. I think he should be able to trust me completely. He needs company and love, he needs someone to listen to him and put up with his moods, and when he is well he simply needs to be treated like a normal human being. I think that he should have attention but not be smothered by it. He needs time and space and quietness in which to work, and someone to act as a barrier between himself and the interferences and pryings of the outside world. On the other hand, if he feels sociable, why not? As long as he can cope. I know that he is most terrified not just of being out of his mind, but of being confined again in any sort of asylum. Whatever the treatment was there – drugs, therapy – it did him no good. Less than no good. But I think I need to be able to give him something when he is very restless and delirious, some sort of sedative. Nine times out of ten he will sleep himself better.'

I sat down. I realized that Meredith had said almost nothing since he arrived, that I was the one who had been talking. It was what I needed. He had seen that.

'You're absolutely right. Of course. He needs security and protection, rather like a child. And watchful attention when he is really ill. Normal human companionship and behaviour towards him for the rest of the time. You must not protect him too much against ordinary life.'

'I think I have been to blame at times in that way.'

'You must not blame yourself, not at all. God knows, none of this is easy, none of us would have failed to make mistakes. I must tell you that from what I've heard I think it unlikely that he will ever get better. There may be quite long spells in between bouts, of course.'

'He was well for two years.'

'Oh yes. The periods may get longer or shorter. It's very hard to say. The point is that if he ever becomes extremely violent, beyond the stage at which you can manage him alone – and if you cannot prevent him from doing injury to himself, or you, or to someone else, then that is a different matter entirely. There might come a time when he would have to be detained in law.'

'Is that inevitable?'

'Nothing in mental illness is inevitable. Whatever you may hear, the truth is that in general we know quite a lot and, in particular cases, perhaps almost nothing. But are you prepared to go on devoting your life to looking after him?'

'Of course.'

'Why? Because you feel you started and cannot choose but go on. Because you see it as a duty?'

'Because I love him.'

He replaced the spectacles. He had a large, pock-marked face, a fleshy nose and his glasses looked out of proportion, comical. But he was a sombre man and he seemed wise and knowledgeable, he had comforted me.

Francis came in, his clothes crumpled, he was rubbing his hair and demanding tea. I had wondered how I might introduce Meredith but in fact there was no need, for Francis at once took it that he was one of my academic colleagues and began to explain to him vociferously that he must persuade me to get on with my book because I needed work of my own to occupy me. Meredith agreed. They got on rather well.

Later in the evening, Francis was standing at the windows looking down on to the snow. There was a frost, the glass was already rimed over with a glistening, foliate pattern.

He said, 'I'm glad you've still got some friends left. I thought I might have driven them all away.'

'No.'

'You must never let that happen.'

'I won't.'

He turned. 'I want to go out for a walk.'

And so we went, for a second time, out into the darkness and the snow.

Meredith had told me that I did right. He upheld me. The doctor in Kerneham had urged me to put Francis into skilled medical hands. And at Battersea, those hands had taken hold of him and wrung him dry, doctors had questioned him until he no longer knew truth from falsehood, they had left him limp and shocked and entirely dispirited from drugs. He would never forget the sights and sounds among which he had been forced to live for those three months, the faces of the mad floated up before his eyes in dreams and in waking, like the hallucinations of a dying man.

The final answer was that we were alone. Francis was alone, he suffered within his own head, and I was alone because he relied upon me and between those differing counsels, between what I suspected and dreaded, hoped and sensed, I had to choose. I felt as though we were the only people left in the world, that night, as we walked through the snow-bound city towards the river, upon which the moon shone, encircled by a ring of frost.

'I don't think I shall ever write anything more. I'm so tired.'

'It doesn't matter just now.'

'No. That's how I know. If I cared about it, I should be working. I don't. Does it matter, if I have said all there is to say?'

'Perhaps not, no.'

'Oh, Harvey, what shall I do? What shall I do with the rest of my life?'

'Rest. Look at things. Read. Eat and sleep.'

'Is it as easy as that then? Have you found out the secret?'

I shook my head. 'It's only what seems best for you now.'

'I have done some good work.'

'Yes.'

'But it isn't much, is it? Not much to look at.'

I touched his arm. 'There will be more. Why are we talking as if you were already dead?' I meant it only to lift him out of his mood. He was leaning far over the stone wall looking down at the river and, for a second, I put out my hand, suddenly regretting what I had said to him, and fearful of what he might do. But I was even more afraid of startling him, the balance in his mind seemed to be as delicate as a scale made for measuring individual grains of sand. But he stood upright again, he seemed fairly calm.

I felt very cold, my face was stinging from the frost.

'There were so many terrible things,' Francis said.

'Shall we start back?'

'The wonders of the world are too much to bear. Those trees and lakes and mountains aren't for people, and all those colours are too bright, your eyes burn. I felt very brittle, as though my bones would break in the wind, my skin might flake off like powder. Don took a photograph of me standing balanced upon a rock at the edge of a lake, with the mountains and trees behind me. I look so insubstantial, you could puff me off the face of the earth. I was very afraid all the time I was there, I thought I would be able to write about it but of course I never shall. While I was there I was trying to be a different person. It was so hard, but I felt for some reason that I ought to try. It deceived me. Everything I saw and read deceived me. I should never have gone.'

'Perhaps it has taught you things about yourself you would never have known.'

'But then there was the voyage home. You can't know what that was like. I can't . . .'

'Francis, we're going to start walking back. Come on.'

I began to lead him, as I had so often done, and he followed me, as he always did. The snow lay thick and stiff, frozen on to walls and railings.

'Well, the poem will come out soon and then they will all sharpen their knives and operate on me, and it will soon be over. They'll forget all about me. It won't take long. It really does not matter if I never write another word.'

'So long as you're happy.'

'Ah. That. Yes.'

He did not speak again for the rest of the way home. That night I sat up for a long time, drinking a glass of brandy, and trying to work out what I·thought, whether Francis was speaking the truth when he said that he would never write again, and whether it mattered or not, to him, to me, to the world in general. I could not imagine what else he might do. A spell of reading and thinking and looking closely at the world about him had only been satisfactory for him before because it led up to a piece of work. I did not think he would be really happy to dawdle through the rest of his life. But America had, as he said, deceived him, put him on the wrong track, and he needed to get over that, to forget whatever had been damaging to him. I did not think he was in a fit state at the moment to make any predictions about the future.

The snow lasted for about another month. During the whole of that time, Francis was unwell, shaky, troubled by nightmares, occasionally suffering from vertigo, which had him clutching at the wall and chairs for support. He had headaches lasting three or four days at a time and he was very depressed in the old way. I had to persuade him to eat, dress, wash, do anything at all except sit in the chair staring blankly ahead of him. I worked away at my long book. We were very dull. Some letters came for him from California but he would not open them. Things could have been much better with us. Francis could have been more energetic and cheerful, he could have been working. But in fact I was touching wood daily that things were no worse.

He was completely indifferent to the forthcoming publication of 'Earth, Air, Water, Fire', Harold Simmons had told him that reactions from those who had read it in proof were the best he had ever received, there was no doubt in anyone's mind now that Francis was a poet of genius. Certainly he was becoming quite widely known and popular, judging by the number of requests for him to lecture here and lunch there, by the praise and gratitude which came to him. He was most pleased either by the opinions of those few writers whose own work he admired, or by letters from everyday readers who had simply enjoyed his poems. These he would always answer with great courtesy. All the rest he dismissed, gave them to me or sent them on to Simmons to deal with. He said, 'It's really nothing to do with me, I can't help them, they should be looking for someone else.'

He spent no time at all in his room at the top of the house, the desk and chair and bookcases gathered dust.

The thaw came, London was dirty, the gutters ran. Crocuses and aconites lay like bright spears of coloured paper in the wet grass. I got home from the British Museum one pouring wet afternoon to find Francis lying on the kitchen floor with his head inside the gas oven.

*

Today I walked as far as the estuary. I would not have believed it possible. I do not believe the words as I write them on to the paper. But the pain in my back and my legs is worse than it has ever been. I sit very close to the fire trying to find a warmth which will seep right through my flesh into my bones and ease them. Much of my life now seems to be taken up with this quest for warmth, for the sun, for hot baths, for fires, for soft, thick blankets and quilts. But in the end it is never sufficient, the cold and the damp are always there, and the aching.

But today, I walked as far as the estuary.

Outside the gate, the path begins. It is narrow and caked hard and dry, running between the tufted grass. It slopes a little and runs straight, and then loops around towards the south-east. It is hot but not too hot, the sun has passed its full summer strength now, there is a hint of mist in the early mornings and white vapour rises over the marshes at night.

On my left, the river. It is very narrow here and the water is as clear as glass and as colourless. On the river bed, pebbles, and sometimes fish, but more often, the detritus of humanity, rusted tins, a blackened shoe.

The weed lies in long, waving strands of a rich spinach-green outspread and floating like the hair of a woman lying in the water. A pair of swans sit motionless on their own pale reflections like hens on their nests.

I walk very slowly. One foot in front of the other. Pause, for the left-hand stick to be pushed forward. Then the second foot and the right-hand stick. It is difficult to lift my feet up properly off the ground, I have to look down at every step for a hidden root, a wide crack, an upturned stone. If I fell here, I should never get myself up, I should lie with the sun shining upon my back. I do not dislike the idea. Perhaps the rays would then have more chance to penetrate my clothing and my skin, to warm me through at last.

The marsh grass is a bright, fresh green, near at hand, but paler in the distance with a yellowish tinge. There are clumps of cow parsley as tall as I am, bleached and dried since the spring to the colour of a ship's biscuit. The seeded heads rattle a little in the wind which blows faintly from off the sea. The reeds are bladed like swords. Ahead of me, the sky fades from blue to white to silver.

The estuary shines and the reflection it sends up into the air gathers together in a radiance like moonlight. As I go nearer and nearer, I see the salt flats, silver-grey, and the knife edge of the sea. Five cormorants cross the sky like witches riding from west to east. In among the reeds at my feet, water rail move about making their harsh, squealing, hissing sounds, dunlin chatter, a redshank flies alone out of nowhere, down into the sedge. I see birds, now that I no longer lie in wait so anxiously for them. My luck has changed. I have waited damp and cramped for hours for the sight of a bittern and strained my eyes through the glasses again and again, thinking to see a tern gliding over the estuary, mistaking it for a gull.

Today, I hear them all, they crowd about me in secret. They are no longer afraid of me. I am one of them, balanced upon my sticks.

It takes me over an hour to reach the mouth of the estuary, I am light-headed with fatigue, I wonder how I shall get back and then dismiss it from my mind. I should be sweating but my skin is dry and salty from the heat of the sun and the marsh wind. The estuary is a tongue of sand and silver spreading out and away. The edges are crowded with flocks of waders and dippers, teeming in among one another. There is a redness about the sun now, a few thin skeins of cloud are pulled like cotton here and there across the sky.

I stand for a long time, resting on my sticks. The estuary is beautiful. Still. Silent. I know that I shall never come here again. My eyes are running a little from the wind, the light wavers and shimmers, as though I am under water, looking up. The light is changing as I watch, becoming yellower.

I turn back and look at the marshes and they spread for miles, a pale wash of green with dark brown islands where the earth shows through.

Francis never came here again. Here, everything is pared down, and when there is no mist or mirage of light, I can see as far as the human eye will ever see. It is lonely. There are the birds.

When I got back, I wondered if I might be going to die. I felt exhausted and entirely content, I felt that I had severed the last of my landlines. But we do not die at the moment when death seems most apt, most welcome. I shall linger on for months or years, failing, weakening, making old bones.

There is very little more to say about Francis. It is thirty years ago today since his death. They have been writing about him again in the literary papers. The young abused him at first but now they are turning to him again, he has become one of their heroes. I have no idea why fashion should now come, now go.

I have only written about three of our twenty years together.

For Francis did not succeed in taking his own life, that March day. I do not think he intended to then, I do not think he was fully aware of what he had tried to do.

I pulled the rolled-up blanket from under the door and turned off the gas, I dragged him out into the passage and opened the front door. There should have been a great gust of air to blow through his lungs to revive him but at first there seemed to be only the sound of the rain and a creeping, soft, moist breath of air. I opened every window in the house. He was pale but he was breathing, his pulse was fairly strong. I telephoned to

Meredith. By the time he had arrived, Francis was conscious and violently sick.

He was in bed for a week. I think he remembered little about what had happened. He became manic for a time then, he roamed about the house shifting books, riffling through papers, dusting everything, he talked incessantly in a stream of non-sense under his breath. I gave him sedatives, which Meredith had prescribed. I stayed with him. Gradually, he calmed down. The cloud passed over.

It was in September of that year that we went to Germany. We took a boat up the Rhine from Mainz and the weather was mild, the forests beautiful, dark green with black hearts. Francis began to work again, he wrote one or two short poems about Venice, bitter poems, heavy with the imagery of rottenness and death, poems which remind me of some Jacobean tragedy of revenge. They stand apart from the rest of his work, they are richer in texture and there is something altogether decadent about them, a corruption rises like steam from off the page.

One weekend, we got off the boat and walked for miles into the forests, to a small village half a mile away from the Schloss Vogel, a rather small, austere castle on high ground overlooking the woods, the Rhine in the distance and, over to the west, flat open countryside. We stayed at an inn in the village and one afternoon walked up the track towards the castle. The air smelled faintly bitter, of pine cones and peat.

Schloss Vogel was empty. It had an inner courtyard and a beautiful and unusual series of small gardens, leading down from one another like stepping stones. There were very many roses and some vines. It was the quietest place I have ever been in my life. There was no movement of air at all, the trees all around were absolutely still, no birds sang.

Francis said, 'I should like to stay here. It would be an abso-lutely new beginning to my life. If I could stay here, my head would never ache so. I could work and be happy.'

We stayed. We rented Schloss Vogel, after letting the house in South Terrace and bringing most of the furniture over to Germany. It looked very small and sparse in those rooms and some of them remained entirely bare for the whole of our life there.

That was, for the next ten years. I think that for those periods when he was well, Francis was happier at Schloss Vogel than he had ever been in his life. He worked a little. He read a little. He walked in the forests for miles, he gardened a great deal. During those years, he became England's most eminent poet. It meant little to him. Because he knew that he would never write anything important again. He had lost the heart and the will, he had no more to say.

But during those years, he was in sound mind for very little of the time. His madness lasted for longer and longer periods, months at a time. It followed, for the most part, the same cycle as before. Except that he was further gone into that world of nightmare and unreason, and there were weeks on end when, although he was amiable enough, I could never reach him. He bought a piano and he would spend hours upstairs crashing up and down the keyboard, or else hammering like a piano tuner on one or two notes, just as he had done that day in Oxford.

He went off into the forest and raved, too, and often I followed him, though it had to be at a distance, he had all the old dread of being spied upon and watched. He would stand and shout a stream of words up into the branches of the trees and wait, his head lifted, as though he were listening to a reply.

He began to be violent towards himself. I had constantly to be on my guard, to keep razor blades and knives and scissors away from him. Twice, he attacked me, once not long after we went there, a swift, almost half-hearted attempt to seize me around the throat, over as soon as it was begun.

But the second time, near the end of our time in Germany, he almost killed me. I was standing at an upstairs window looking down over the tops of the trees towards the river, when he came upon me and tried to push me out and, for a split second, I lost my balance and the world reeled, I was almost over the edge. But somehow, I managed to force myself back against Francis and topple him away. He hit his head on the arm of a heavy chair as he went down and bled rather badly. I knelt beside him, my heart pounding, trying not to faint from shock and from terror that he was dead, that in trying to kill me he had killed himself.

That time, he remembered what he had done, he wept like a child and I could not comfort him.

Somehow, I was never afraid, I did not go about the house braced for an attack, I did not glance over my shoulder or refrain from turning my back on him. I had long ceased to wonder whether he would get better or worse. I knew that he could only get worse. I had several times renewed my promise to him that I would never send him into an asylum. It became a good day, if he had some rest, if I persuaded him to eat, if he would let me read to him for a while, or if he was simply upstairs for hours, hitting the piano, making his own harsh, mad music.

I was happy at Schloss Vogel, in spite of it all. I did not want to leave. I did not know how I could explain to Francis that we must leave. By 1935, it was clear to me, although we lived a remote life here, that we should have to get out. The letters which reached me from London begged me to do so.

During a few days, when Francis was comparatively well, we packed up, and returned to South Terrace. I was filled with relief, and filled with misery, for I knew that we should never find such peace in a place again.

We went to Kerneham. That was the best I could do for us. London was impossible for Francis, I could not keep close enough watch upon him, and I did not want anyone to see him, if it could be avoided.

But the secret was out. The world knew, now, that Francis was mad. Life at Kerneham continued in the same way, except that things were worse, infinitely worse.

And then, one late afternoon in the summer, I found him gone, he had left the cottage, he was not in the village, the search of years before began again. Except that he was not far away, and I knew where to go. He was in the church. I had tried to keep everything away from him. I had not thought of the secateurs. It was the priest whom I fetched first of all, he came with me and we knelt down and prayed in that cold, stone building, over Francis's body and, when I stood up, I saw that my trousers were soaked through with his blood.

There is nothing else to tell. I returned to London. The war had begun. I worked in the Far Eastern translations department of the War Ministry. After the war, I returned to my old post at the British Museum. I lived a solitary, industrious, purposeless life. I retired. I came to live here. Nothing more.

There is only one thing left to do now. I am tired, I am very tired.

I have the papers all here. The black notebooks, the manuscripts, the letters. I carry them over to the fireplace which is very wide and glowing, piled high with logs. Mrs Mumford makes a good fire. I have tended it carefully all evening.

I sit on the edge of the low chair and pull it up close to the grate, and then I feed the books one by one into the depths of the flames, pressing them down with the poker. It takes a long time. My eyes are smarting from the smoke. But at last they are all gone. I drop the final, crumpled sheet on to the flames and it is licked up and consumed at once. I wait until the fire dies down and then riddle the ashes through until they fall like dust down between the bars of the grate.

Now I have finished. I have kept my promise.

There are no papers.

Aldeburgh, March 1972